SECRETS NEAR GOLDFINCH GAP

NICOLETTE HARPFORD

This book is a work of fiction. All events, characters, businesses, locations and related material are solely from the author's imagination. Any similarity between the content of this text and any event, person, living or dead, business or location is coincidental.

Copyright © 2024 by Nicolette Harpford

PRINT ISBN-13: 979-8-9876688-2-5

Cover Design: BookCoverZone

Editor: M. Perez

Edition: First

Printing: Second

Published by Avenue du Gui

CONTENTS

CHAPTER ONE

DAVY PINESMITH

A river of coffee flows across my desk, dyeing part of my yellow legal pad a rusty brown and soaking through a stack of envelopes before coming to a stop right at the edge of my laptop.

"I just poured that too!" Mr. Hawking, my editor, grumbles.

He had placed his mug on my desk while on the way to the bathroom, and my desk happens to be right next to the toilets. When I was first hired at the magazine, the only desk open was this one. At the time, I hadn't complained, but now, several years later, I wouldn't mind a relocation. The trouble is Mr. Hawking doesn't usually interact with me unless he needs to set something on my desk while sprinting to the restroom.

"At least I didn't get anything on my shirt. Nothing is worse than a scolding from Mrs. Hawking." Mr. Hawking picks up his almost empty mug.

I bite my tongue. Mr. Hawking hasn't noticed that while his shirt is spotless, the coffee is splashed across his pants. He's a bit accident prone when it comes to food and beverages. It's only thirty minutes past eight, and the coffee on my desk isn't even the first food-related event of the morning (the first one involved an éclair and a very unhappy receptionist who had to make an emergency hair appointment).

"That reminds me. Emma, I'm going to need your article for "The Backyard Bird Blurb" by the end of the day," a dribble of coffee slides down Mr. Hawking's chin as he talks.

"I turned it in yesterday morning," I say to Mr. Hawking's retreating back. I doubt that he heard me.

"The Backyard Bird Blurb" is found in every issue of *The Binocular Feather Feature Birding Magazine* (or *The BFF Birding Magazine* as our readers call it—I'm still amazed that someone would give a magazine such a long, unnecessary title). It's the one article in the magazine I'm assigned to consistently, and the one article in the magazine no one really cares about. It involves a short writeup about a common songbird that most our readers can spot in their own gardens. The article I've been working on most recently is about purple finches.

As much as I enjoy writing "The Backyard Bird Blurb," it's not exactly the type of journalism I envision devoting myself to long term. The problem is Mr. Hawking rarely remembers to give me any assignments, and if I ever want to permanently leave "The Backyard Bird Blurb" behind and become one of the top writers for the magazine, Mr. Hawking needs to know that I can handle the big stories. But how can I show him that I'm up for the job when I almost never get assigned anything interesting? It has been months since my last notable article. It's as if Mr. Hawking forgets I work for the magazine most of the time.

My computer loudly pings at my desk, disturbing the quiet office. Penelope Gray, one of the magazine's top photojournalists who sits nearby, gives me a dirty look. I quickly mute the sound on my computer, and mouth sorry to her. She rolls her eyes and goes back to editing something on her screen. I don't take it personally. I worked with her this past winter on a story, and while she was a bit prickly at first, I soon learned that she just has a funny way of treating her friends.

Navigating over to my email inbox, I see that I have a new message titled *Urgent Opportunity*. I sit up eagerly and lean my elbows onto the desk where my sleeves become saturated in lukewarm coffee, but I don't care. I hardly ever get emails like this. I click the message and the email loads onto the screen.

It's a grainy picture of two older men fly fishing. One has large, round cheeks and a gummy smile while the other scowls at the camera with sharp wrinkles marking his worn skin. His facial expression reminds me of Penelope a bit. There's no text attached to the email or any context to the strange picture. Looks like the email is junk and not a career-changing story to write. Suddenly, the coffee that has seeped into my sleeves feels cold and sticky.

I spend the rest of the morning trying to explain to the graphics department why they can't use a photograph of a house finch on my purple finch "Backyard Bird Blurb" spread despite how similar the two birds look. Finally, the lead designer agrees to use the correct photograph. As I leave, I catch the beginnings of a conversation about how all birds look the same and how it wouldn't hurt if some of the writers at the magazine got out a bit more.

Back at my desk, I skim through my email inbox and find a second email marked *Urgent Opportunity.* This time I don't sit up high in my seat in anticipation. If I had to bet, I would say I'll probably find another random photograph sent to the wrong email address. Maybe this one will be of the fish the men caught.

The email loads slowly, but unlike the last one, words appear on the screen.

Dear Miss Emma Finch,

I've read a few articles you've written in the past year, and I've been impressed with your work. I was hoping you would visit me on my farm for a day or two and interview me for your magazine. My name is Davy Pinesmith. You might not know who I am because I was a bit before your time, but I was a folk singer back in my heyday.

If you don't believe me, look me up on your internet. I've been told that there are old videos of me on there and even some encyclopedia entries. Anyways, the 60th anniversary of the release of my most famous song, "Goldfinch of My Heart," is this week, and I know that magazine of yours specializes in birds and things related to them.

If you do choose to come down for a visit, let me know. I can set up a cabin for you.

With kind words and thoughts,

Davy Pinesmith

P.S. I know it's spring, but you'll want to pack for cooler weather since you'll be up in the mountains.

P.P.S. I also sent you a photograph so that you could verify my identity. I sent it in an earlier email.

I read the email twice before I can process its contents. I've never heard of this Davy Pinesmith guy before, and the email is more than a bit odd, but I'm not in a position to be fussy about articles. If I write one more piece about the best type of seed to put in a birdfeeder, I might lose my mind.

It doesn't take more than a minute before my internet search shows that the scowling man from the photograph in the earlier email is Davy Pinesmith and that he is indeed a big deal. It isn't difficult to find information about him or his music. He's had three biographies written about him, and one of them was even turned into a made-for-TV movie. There are multiple fan sites associated with him along with an official website run by a large record label. There are even black and white videos of him performing at large festivals back in the day.

My lips tug up into a smile. I can hear my heart beating to the tune of *cover story.* I forward the email to Mr. Hawking and head straight for his office. Who knew the tides could change on such short notice? Maybe today won't end up being that bad.

"Is something wrong?" Mr. Hawking asks when I appear in his doorway.

He has refilled his coffee mug since I last saw him, and some of the brown liquid slops out onto his shirt as he takes a sip.

"I actually have great news," I say. I can't help beaming.

"You're finally done writing "The Backyard Bird Blurb?" Emma, you know, you don't have to come to my office to tell me that. You can just send an email."

A moment ago, I would've been peeved that Mr. Hawking still hadn't realized that my article had been sitting in his inbox for more than 24 hours, but that doesn't seem to matter anymore. I might just have the interview that makes my career.

"I forwarded you an email. A folk singer by the name of Davy Pinesmith has asked me to interview him."

Mr. Hawking's eyes widen. "Davy Pinesmith! *The* Davy Pinesmith?"

I nod my head. "He said he wrote a song titled "Goldfinch of My Heart" sixty years ago, and he wants to do an interview about it on his farm. He looks like the real deal based on what I saw online."

"You shouldn't have to search the internet to know that Davy Pinesmith is the real deal! I grew up listening to his music. I think I was only a tot when "Goldfinch of My Heart" came out. In fact, Mrs. Hawking and I danced to that exact song when we got married."

"So, I can go?"

"*Can* you go? You *must* go." Mr. Hawking shuffles a few pieces of papers around his desk. "When did he say you needed to be there?"

"He didn't exactly say I had to go at a certain time, but he did mention this week is the anniversary of "Goldfinch of My Heart.""

"We will need you to get down there as soon as possible then. Reply to his email and tell him that you can be there tomorrow morning." Mr. Hawking smiles to himself and begins to hum a tune as he flips through an agenda book. "I can't believe we've got an interview with Davy Pinesmith," he whispers to himself. "His song is one of the highest charting songs about birds of all time. Our readers will eat it up!"

Back at my desk, I send an email back to Davy Pinesmith, telling him that I would be more than glad to come and visit him. As soon as I hit send though, the small smile that has made itself comfortable on my face is whisked away.

This weekend I had made plans to have a picnic with Harry Starling, my almost-boyfriend. We had been seeing each other for some time now, but he had yet to ask me to be his girlfriend officially. He worked for a private investigation firm that was always sending him on projects to gather evidence surrounding peculiar cold cases, so sometimes our schedules didn't align well. He had gone out of his way to make sure we would see each other this weekend, which had led me to suspect he was going to make our relationship official over a romantic picnic in the park.

I can't tell Mr. Hawking that though. I'll just have to hope that my visit to see Davy Pinesmith doesn't extend into the weekend and that I can score a quick interview. If everything goes to plan, this could end up being the perfect weekend.

It doesn't take long for Davy Pinesmith to reply to my email and confirm he'll have a cabin ready for me near his farm by sunset in a few days' time (his words, not mine). Mr. Hawking is ecstatic. He even gives me a small stipend for gas and food and writes down his personal cellphone number on a piece of paper so that I can reach him at all times. Around lunch, I even catch him printing out a copy of the email I forwarded to him and pinning it up on the community bulletin board in the breakroom. Who knew that a random email would be so great for my journalism career? Davy Pinesmith might just become my new favorite musician.

Chapter Two

Off to Adventure

My ears pop as the highway weaves its way into the hilly scenery. The mountains form smooth, green waves with splashes of pink and white from the spring blossoms. I'm on my way to visit Davy Pinesmith, and while the magazine office is located in a relatively small town, I have a feeling that the area where Davy grew up will be minuscule. For the last half hour, the largest town I passed had a sign stating its population was just under 4,000.

By the time I take my exit to enter a place called Sourwood, the sun is just starting to slip behind the tops of the nearby mountains. The town is tiny with a few scattered buildings, shops and a small number of houses lining the main road. Beyond these structures, farmland stretches until it meets the tree-dense hills. I find a spot on the side of the road to pull over so that I can check my email on my cellphone. I'll be staying in a rental that Davy arranged for me. He had sent me special instructions about reaching the cabin just the other day.

Based on the map he attached to the email, I don't think the cabin will be too difficult to find. There are only a handful of country lanes bridging off the main road of the town, and the cabin that he's reserved for my stay looks to be only a turn away.

Just as I'm putting my phone away, it rings. I check the screen and see that my mother is calling. While I love my parents, I rarely see them since they have chosen to spend their retirement traveling the world and living on cruise ships when they can't find a friend to let them couch surf. I try to never miss one of their calls since I never know when I'll hear from them again.

"Hey, Mom," I answer the phone.

"Emma, you'll never believe it," my mother's loud voice shouts through the speaker. "Your dad thinks he saw your third cousin, Gary, on the cruise we're on. We just disembarked, and I had to call you and tell you."

"Gary?" I ask. My father's family happens to be exuberantly large, and my mother is always convinced that his relatives are popping up on every inch of the globe.

"Yes, Gary! He has glasses, lots of hair. I think he studied fish at university...or was it fishing? The two seem so similar," she takes a deep breath to continue, but I cut her off before she can go on a tangent.

"Mom, I have to go. I'm staying at a cabin for a few days, and I want to get there before it gets dark. I haven't exactly been to this area before."

"Is this another work assignment? How exciting!" Mom takes a pause before lowering her voice, "Just try not to get in trouble again. You don't want them thinking you're a magnet for murder at the magazine."

"Mom!" Heat flushes my cheeks.

"I'm just speaking the truth, Emma. The last few times you've gone out of town for work, someone has shown up dead."

"Those were both very odd, coincidental events, and the people responsible were caught both times."

My mother is referencing the articles I wrote about *Nuthatch Nest*, an old home my great aunt owned, and *The Starling Statue*, a magnificent sculpture that was enshrined with mystery. While I was working on both assignments, I happened to get entangled in murder plots. The likelihood of something like that happening again would be ridiculous.

Someone shouts *tequila* and pumping music can be heard in the background on my mother's end of the line. "I have to go. Your father looks like he's about to get up to something. Talk to you later." The phone clicks.

When the call screen closes, I see that I have a new text message from Harry. After Mr. Hawking confirmed that I would be working on the story about Davy Pinesmith, I had sent Harry a text about my plans to stay in Sourwood along with an apology if my work ended up interfering with our weekend plans (which I was still hoping it wouldn't).

I open the text message and my heart swings into my stomach. All Harry has sent is the word *cool*. That can't be good. I knew he'd be disappointed if something came up this weekend, but I expected him to be somewhat understanding given how crazy his own work schedule is. Not only that, but a one-word response to my thoughtful message feels a bit like Harry doesn't really care about our plans at all. Maybe I have been misreading our situation this whole time. Maybe I was still just some girl Harry took on a date once in a blue moon.

I don't bother to reply and shove my phone deep into my purse. Out of sight out of mind. At least that's what I say to myself as I put the vehicle in drive and make my way to the small country lane that will lead to the cabin. The road is rough and filled with potholes, but the driveway of the cabin is easy to spot. It's not long before I'm unloading my luggage and walking up the steps that lead to the front door.

Inside the cabin, there is a dual living room and kitchen area. It's small, but it has everything I'll need to be comfortable for a few days. There's a round table, painted dark blue, under a window surrounded by three wooden chairs. On top of the table, one yellow rose has been placed in a simple glass vase. Next to the table, there is some counterspace along with a sink and minifridge. On the other side of the room, there are two recliners with well-worn plaid cloth and an area rug that matches the blue table. The armchairs are situated so that they face a black wood stove. Despite the cramped quarters, the room makes me want to curl up with a good book and a cup of peppermint tea. Maybe this little stint in the mountains will be just the type of work retreat that I need to refresh.

I roll my suitcase into the nearby bedroom and find it to be as cozy as the other part of the cabin. There's a carmine-colored rug covering the hardwood floors and a bed in a rustic, wooden frame. I plop myself onto the mattress and find that it's not too soft yet not too firm. I don't think I'll have a problem wrapping myself up in the quilt and slipping into sleep later tonight.

I unpack the things in my suitcase, and when I'm done, I pull out my notebook and a book I bought about Davy Pinesmith before making myself comfortable in one of the recliners by the wood stove. After I emailed Davy to let him know that I would be on my way to Sourwood, he suggested I come over to his farm in the morning after I was settled in, so there's no point in wandering about now that the stars are starting to come out.

I flip through the biography and study some of the photographs in the back of the novel. There are several photographs of Davy playing his guitar on stage and singing in a studio, but the one the strikes me the most is of him standing in front of an old barn with a young woman who has hair that rests at her waist. She's dressed in a flowy skirt and wearing a crown of flowers on her head. The caption below tells me it is a photograph taken with his sister, Matilda.

I flip to the front of the book and make it about half way through the first chapter before my eyes grow heavy. Soon, the words grow fuzzy on the pages, so I set the book down on an end table and retire for the night. I fall asleep listening to the sounds of the woods nearby.

CHAPTER THREE

THE EMPTY FARMHOUSE

There are no warm hues of orange streaking the sky, only heavy, gray clouds when I pull into 15 Goldfinch Gap Lane to meet with Davy Pinesmith. The farm itself is smaller than I imagined. In my mind, I pictured rolling fields that stretched into the mountains and a sturdy red structure accompanied by a pair of silos, but the reality is far from that. A simple, rectangular farmhouse in need of a new coat of paint sits at the end of the gravel driveway next to the bones of an old, wooden barn that looks like a heavy wind could carry it away into the nearby forest.

I climb up the lopsided steps and knock on the door. Nearby, a mourning dove coos and a small animal rustles about in a derelict flowerbed. Otherwise, the farm is quiet. I hope Davy hasn't forgotten about our interview. Even if he has, I'm not about to go back to Mr. Hawking empty handed, especially not after seeing how excited he was. I settle in on the steps and decide I'll just wait a bit before I leave. Maybe Davy is taking his morning shower or out in the woods. Perhaps, he went into town to grab something. There doesn't appear to be any vehicles around, and I doubt the old barn could hide a car.

I pull my phone out and read the daily news after I complete a crossword puzzle and check my text messages. I don't have any new ones from Harry. Best to leave that situation alone for now. I need to stay focused if I want to make a good impression on Davy, even if he doesn't seem to be too concerned with making a positive impression on me.

He had sounded so kind and excited in his emails, so I'm surprised that he would forget that we were meeting today. The thought makes me fret. What if something happened to him? The farmhouse stands two stories high and looks to be from another century. What if he fell down the stairs and needs help? I chew my lip and let a couple minutes pass, but the thought won't leave my head. What could it hurt if I peek inside?

I walk over to the flowerbed and stand on my tippy-toes to get a good look inside of the house. The kitchen is barren with a single table and a collection of chairs missing several legs. It is definitely not the type of place I imagined a famous singer residing in.

"What are you doing in my begonia bed?" A gruff voice asks from behind me, making me jump.

A man with a weatherworn face stands in the gravel drive wearing a straw hat that looks like it needs to be replaced. His jeans are ripped, and by the looks of his shirt, he has been working outside. Grass stains and dirt cover one of the sleeves. He looks just like the photograph he sent me.

"Why are you still standing in my begonias?" Davy asks.

"I'm so sorry," I step out of the flowerbed. "It's wonderful to finally meet you. I didn't mean to intrude. I was just wondering where you were."

The stern wrinkle running between his eyes deepens. "You were wondering where I was? Why would you be wondering that?"

I let out a nervous laugh. This meeting isn't going the way I thought it would. "For the interview. You told me to meet you here, at your farm."

Davy shakes his head. "I haven't given anyone an interview in about twenty years, and I certainly have no plans to start now. I suggest you get off my property before I call the sheriff." Davy points at my car. I notice that there's a small trickle of blood lacing its way between his fingers. "And get that car off my lot too."

I awkwardly scurry into my vehicle and pull onto the road as fast as I can. I watch him glare at me in the review mirror the whole time. My heart thumps against my chest so hard that my seatbelt feels tight. I've heard of other journalists who are digging for a story having to deal with aggressive people and intimidation before, but those were all for investigative, hard-hitting crime articles. Not the type of stuff usually published in a birding magazine.

I end up on the main street of Sourwood, looking for a coffee shop or any place where I can take a moment to figure out a new game plan. I would drive back to the cabin, but it's on the other side of the town, and I'm a bit nervous returning to the property now that Davy might not even want me here. Obviously, something has gone very wrong. Davy invited me here to interview him about the anniversary of his song "Goldfinch of My Heart," even going as far as to rent a cabin for me, but when I show up at his house for the interview, he threatens to call the police and claims he has never agreed to an interview?

I pull my car into a spot in front of a place called Country Time Coffee. I grab my notebook and a pen and head inside. The shop smells overwhelmingly of bitter coffee beans mixed with sweet pastries. It's fairly empty except for a woman working behind the counter. She's humming along to a song on the radio while she reads the newspaper. She sees me standing at the cash register and shoves the newspaper out of the way.

"Hope you haven't been standing there long. What can I get you?" She looks at me with round, blue eyes. Her auburn hair is frizzy and matches the disorganization of the shop.

"Can I get a latte?"

"Sure thing," she taps on the register screen.

I pass her a few bills and take a seat at the front of the shop so that I can look out the window that faces the street. A mail truck rumbles by as I run through my options in my head. I could call Mr. Hawking and tell him what's happened, but then he might think I can't handle the story, and that's the last thing I need him to think. I could pack up my things and go back to the office and make up a story about why I couldn't get the interview, but then not only would Mr. Hawking think I can't deliver on my articles, I would also be a liar, so definitely not that option. I don't even know why that one came to mind.

The bells on the door jingle and a spry man dressed in a tan uniform and thick, matching coat walks in and orders a coffee with sugar at the register. After he orders, he turns to look at me, and I see that his face doesn't match his body as he's much older than I anticipated. Despite his rounded cheeks, he has sagging jowls and thinning, gray hair. Something about him piques my interest, but I can't figure out why. He notices me looking at him and turns bright red before hastily turning around.

"Here you go, Sheriff," the woman with the auburn hair hands him a cup of coffee. I notice it's not a to-go cup, so he must be on his break.

"Thanks, dear," he looks at the cup. "Actually, could I get this to go. Need to get a move on." He peers back at me before turning around again.

The barista lets out a hearty laugh. "Sheriff, why are you acting so odd? You and I both know you take your break at the same time and in the same place every day." The woman's face turns grave. "Did something happen again?"

"No, no," the sheriff appears flustered. "I just have to get going. Anyways, that's all."

I swear his eyes dart in my direction again. It's not my imagination. The barista sees it too. She puts her hands on her wide hips and stares at the sheriff. She doesn't say a word, but I can tell the look she's giving him is one that no one in this town wants to be on the other end of.

"Now that I've had a second to think, I actually think I will take my coffee in here," the sheriff's words stumble over his tongue. "I've got a lot to think about today though with everything going on in town, so don't bother me, Beatrice."

Beatrice raises her eyebrows, but she doesn't say anything.

The sheriff takes the table across from mine and sits down in the seat facing away from me so that I'm looking at his back. His face appears in the reflection of the window glass, and I study it, trying to figure out why it looks familiar. The woman who the sheriff called Beatrice comes over and sets a latte on my table. She gives me a friendly smile before going back behind the counter and humming a tune again as she busies herself. I recognize the song as "Goldfinch of My Heart." I shake my head at the irony. I wonder if she knows Davy Pinesmith lives only a moment from here.

I look back at the sheriff's reflection, and that's when everything comes together. The sheriff is the man from the photograph that Davy had sent me over email! The two men must be friends. I bet he could help me figure out why Davy invited me here for an interview and now won't give me one.

I get up from my table and go and stand in front of the sheriff. He just about spits his coffee out when he sees me standing in front of him.

"Can I help you, Miss?" he averts his eyes.

"Actually, yes. My name is Emma Finch. I'm a reporter for a magazine, and I was invited down here to interview a local man named Davy Pinesmith."

A hearty laugh chimes out in the café. Beatrice is keeled over, laughing. "Hope that's just a joke. I've never heard of anyone being able to have polite small talk with Davy Pinesmith let alone get an interview out of that old grump."

The sheriff shifts uncomfortably in his seat. "Now, that's not true. I'm friends with the fellow."

"You and only you," says Beatrice as she goes back to her newspaper.

The sheriff lets out a long sigh before taking an equally long sip of his coffee. "You better sit down. I have some explaining to do."

Chapter Four

THE SHERIFF'S STORY

T he sheriff takes another sip of his coffee and clears his throat before he leans across the table towards me. There's no one in the coffee shop except us and Beatrice, but his body language acts otherwise. "I'll start at the very beginning. My wife is a big birder. Loves sitting out on the porch and watching whatever comes by. We've got more feeders than I can count. Anyways, she reads that magazine you work for. I always know when the mailman has delivered a new issue because she'll come running inside yelling *my BFF is here*. The grandkids find it something funny because *BFF* means best friends forever to them.

"I read a little bit here and there. I like nature too, so I'm not above educating myself with a nature magazine. Usually, I don't find the articles too interesting, no offense," he holds his hand up in apology. "But recently, I was reading one of the old issues when the cable went out, and I saw one of your articles. It was about some old house named after a bird, Nut Bird House or something or other, and I got to reading it and at the end, you solved a murder. You know which one I'm talking about?"

I nod as a flush runs up my neck and pricks of perspiration tickle my forehead. I know that the sheriff is referencing the time when Mr. Hawking sent me out to write a story about *Nuthatch Nest*, but I'm not understanding how any of it could possibly be connected to Davy kicking me off his farm.

"Anyways, I've been sheriff around here a long time. It might surprise you to know, but I'm getting up there in age. My wife says I don't look a day past 45, and she's never lied to me, but what most don't know is that I could be drawing full social security."

I nod my head again, not sure what to say. The sheriff definitely looks older than 45. He looks more like father time than a strapping young man. His wife either really loves him or needs a visit to the optometrist.

"Ever since I became the sheriff in Sourwood, we've only had a handful of crimes. Most of these were small things. Pranks at the local high school gone wrong, a small scuffle after a football game, things like that. My whole career, I only ever worked one big crime, and it happened long ago. It was unfortunate, and I remember hoping I'd never have to work one like that again. Up until a couple weeks ago, I thought I never would."

I notice that Beatrice hasn't flipped the newspaper she's been reading for quite some time. She's most likely eavesdropping. I lean in towards the sheriff. "What happened recently?"

The sheriff takes another lengthy sip of his coffee and leans back in his chair. "Murder."

"Around here?" I ask, astonished. Sourwood is such a quiet and quaint town. It is hard to envision it as the setting of a murder.

"Found a body in the woods not far from here. I'm the only full timer in the town, so I had to call in some nearby units. They assisted in the beginning, but in the end, they said I had to figure out what happened myself." The sheriff finishes his coffee. "I did my fair share of work for a bit, but I realized I needed help, and that's when I came across your article."

My eyebrows furrow. "Did you send me an email pretending to be Davy Pinesmith just to get me to come here and help you?" I squeeze my hands together under the table. "No wonder Davy told me to get off his property. He probably thought I was trespassing."

The sheriff's round cheeks turn a deep red. "I didn't know what else to do! None of the others around here can help. I had to give it a try. Davy happens to be from Sourwood, and he also happened to have a famous song about a bird, I figured I would give it a chance. And, I'm sure happy I did because look where we are. Sitting next to each other sipping coffee."

"I'm flattered and all, but I can't help you. The only reason I was able to solve that other murder was because I was working with a detective," I say in reference to Harry. I stand and zip up my light coat. "I think I should get going. Thank you for putting me up in that cabin, but I think I should leave."

"You did such a good job in that article I read," the sheriff pauses. "But if you can't do it, you can't do it. I just didn't take you for a liar, that's all."

"A liar?" I choke out the words. I'm not sure what the sheriff is on about, but I know I'm not a liar.

"Well, that must be why you won't help me. If your newspaper article was true, you wouldn't be so scared to give me a hand."

The sheriff stands up and brushes off his pants. "The cabin I got you is paid for, so you might as well enjoy it. Sourwood is a fine town. There's not a lot to do, but there's lots of nice people." He opens the door to the coffee shop and looks back at me one last time. "If you do change your mind and decide that you can give me and this town a little bit of help, I can usually be found at my office across the street."

CHAPTER FIVE

THE CHEESE

The pink buds of a spindly tree knock against the window in the light noon breeze. After my conversation with the sheriff, I went back to the cabin. I needed a moment to think about what I should do. There was no way that I could show back up at the magazine without a story. Mr. Hawking might let me go right on the spot. And if he did keep me hired on, he probably would never consider me for a big story again.

As I pace, I fiddle with my cellphone. It would help if I had someone to talk to, but my parents are halfway around the world, and Harry doesn't seem to have a drop of interest in me. Even the thought of him makes my already upset stomach churn. There are my coworkers, but they might tell Mr. Hawking that I lost the Davy Pinesmith story, and I can't let that happen.

The sheriff had said he was friends with Davy. Maybe if I agreed to help him, I could strike some sort of deal to get my interview. That would be ridiculous though. How am I supposed to help solve a murder? Sure, I have done it before, but both times had been out of necessity, and to be frank, most of my breaks in those cases had come in the form of good timing. Not only that, but I don't want to work with someone who called me a liar.

My stomach lets off a growl, and I remember that I haven't eaten anything all day. I need to pick up some groceries in town if I'm to last the rest of the week, let alone the day. I grab my keys and head out to my car. The light wind has blown teardrop-shaped blossoms onto the window of my car. I go to open the driver door when I notice something that looks like a paper stuck on the windshield. Odd, considering that my cabin is removed far from town.

I grab the paper, but it feels rough in my hand. When I turn over the white parchment, I discover that it is actually a piece of birch bark. Above my car, the skinny, white limb of a birch tree extends. It's the first tree of its kind that I've seen in the area.

When I get in the car, I place the bark on the passenger seat and head into town. There's no grocery store on the narrow main street, so I settle for a pharmacy next to the coffee shop I visited earlier. I'm not disappointed in my choice. Inside, the aisles are filled with local foods and products. It doesn't take long for me to fill a cart up with farm fresh eggs, vegetables, and locally baked bread. If I'm not careful, the stipend that Mr. Hawking gave me will evaporate before my eyes.

As I near the back of the shop, a pungent and putrid smell fills my nose. Maybe I should put my food items back and just see if the coffee shop sells sandwiches. It might not be the wisest to buy food in a place permeating with the odor of rot. I'm just about to turn my cart around when I hear a familiar voice.

"I drove for some time to get here, and now that I'm here, you're telling me you're out of stock? This is the only place in the country where I can get this cheese." A man with dark hair, threaded with silver, talks to a worker. "I can smell the cheese. Surely, you can't deprive me of it? I spent hours trying to find this place. The least you could do is tell me the next time you are getting a shipment."

The worker, who appears to be no older than sixteen, shrugs his shoulders. "Sorry, man. I just take the stuff out of the boxes and put 'em on the shelves."

"This isn't just *stuff*. It's soft cheese covered in a cranberry and apple cinnamon crust with a fig at its center. Where else could I find this cheese?" The man desperately pleads.

I take a step forward. "Charlie Kim? Is that you?" I ask.

The man begging for the cheese turns to look at me, and his face lights up with a huge smile. Charlie is a friend of mine who happens to be a well-known food critic. He makes his living traveling around the country trying odd foods and writing about them for major publications.

"Emma Finch? Who knew that this world would bring us together again! And to the tiny mountain town of Sourwood of all places!" Charle seems to forget the worker and embraces me in a friendly hug.

"I'm here for a story, or rather, I *was* here for a story."

Charlie glances at the front of the shop where the worker has retreated and is talking to the manager. "You aren't alone in your boat. I also *was* here for a story, but now that there's no cheese, my story is a bust too."

"That's a bummer," I say. "The cabin I'm staying in is good for a while, so even though my story seems to be going nowhere, I plan on sticking around. It couldn't hurt." I don't bother to mention the sheriff's bizarre offer to me to help solve a murder.

The young worker Charlie had been talking to reappears. "My manager says we're getting another shipment soon. He says to check back daily and in the morning." The young worker leans in towards Charlie and lowers his voice to a whisper, "Honestly, man, the stuff smells so bad you could probably just drive by the shop with your windows down and that would tell you if the cheese was in stock."

The worker slaps a hand on Charlie's back and saunters away while Charlie stares after him with a look of horror.

"Sometimes I worry for the youth. If they can't identify a good cheese by now, they might never be able to," Charlie shakes his head as if the young man who works in the shop is bound for a life of trials and tragedies.

He turns back to me. "Well, it looks like I'll be in town for a few days as well."

Charlie and I stand in the driveway of his rental cabin which looks more like a house that should be on the cliffy beaches of Malibu than in the mountains near Sourwood. It turns out that the person who the sheriff rented my cabin from owns several others throughout Sourwood, and Charlie managed to reserve one that is larger than mine, and by the looks of it, a lot pricier. Along with possessing sharp corners and never-ending windows, the cabin is built high up in the hills and has an intricate deck that overlooks a vast swath of green forestland. When Charlie had asked me to check out his rental with him, I jumped at the chance. Now that I don't have an interview with Davy, I don't have much else to do in Sourwood.

"I have emergency luggage in my car for reasons exactly like this," Charlie says to me as he pops the trunk open and pulls out a blue roller suitcase.

Charlie looks up at the steep, wooden staircase that leads to the front door. "Maybe I should invest in an emergency duffle bag instead of rolling luggage. It would make situations like this a little more pleasant."

He goes ahead of me and drags his suitcase up the stairs, knocking every step as he goes. Once at the front door, he enters a keycode and unlocks the door. Unlike my cabin, Charlie's cabin is large and airy. The wood floors and smooth walls aren't dark like mine, but instead, they're stained a soothing gray.

"This is amazing," I say as I run my hand along the granite counters in the kitchen.

Charlie shrugs his shoulders. "It'll have to do until that cheese shipment gets in." He lets out a sigh. "I've seen worse."

While Charlie unpacks his suitcase in the nearby bedroom, I flip through the guestbook that's been placed on a table next to the front door. My cabin has one too, but I haven't had time to read through it. Before I can get very far though, Charlie comes back into the room. He fills up a glass of water from the sink and leans against the counter.

"So, what should we do? I can't remember the last time I took a mountain vacation."

It's my turn to shrug my shoulders. "I'm probably going to spend time trying to get one of the locals to give me an interview. I can't go back to work without an article."

"That's right," Charlie says, "you said you came here for a story. What happened?"

I hesitate to tell Charlie about the sheriff and the trick that was played on me, but I've known Charlie for a while, and it's not like I have anyone else to talk to about my problem. I explain to him the email that was sent to me, what happened when I visited Davy Pinesmith, and my peculiar run-in with the sheriff in town.

"I guess I don't really know what to do from here," I say.

Charlie sets his drinking glass down. "I think it's obvious."

"It is?" I ask.

"You're going to help the sheriff solve a murder, but on one condition: he'll get you an interview with this folk singer."

Chapter Six

A Visit to the Sheriff's

Originally, I chuckle at Charlie's suggestion, but it isn't long before he fully convinces me that helping the sheriff is the right thing to do. Before I know it, the two of us are back in town, standing in front of the sheriff's office. It's located in a small building that is towered over by a vacant shop leaning a bit to one side. A worn sign sticks out from above the door that says *Sourwood Sheriff*. It's exactly where the sheriff said it would be when I spoke to him at the coffee shop.

Charlie opens the door for me and gestures for me to enter first with a gallant bow. There's a desk next to a couple of flags, a few chairs in front of that, and four walls, each covered with posters that say things like *A Fire Ban Means No Fires!* and *Out of Season Means No Hunting!* A boyish grin spreads across Charlie's face as he points to one near the door. *Don't Poke the Local Bears!*

"I wonder why the town felt the urge to print that one?" Charlie raises his eyebrows.

I smile back. "I wonder how you're supposed to tell if they are local or just visiting."

One of two doors behind the desk opens, and the sheriff appears. He doesn't seem to notice that Charlie and I are in the room as he limps to his desk with his hand on his lower back.

"Darn seat is too low," he mumbles under his breath as he gets comfortable in his chair.

Once settled, he glances up and sees Charlie waiting in front of the desk.

"Hello!" He quickly stands from his seat, but whatever pain had been bothering him must return because he lets out a yowl before plunking himself back in the chair.

"Sorry about the wait," he says to Charlie as he shuffles through some papers. "I have a hard time hearing if anyone is out here while I'm in the bathroom. The missus thinks I need some hearing aids, but she's full of silly ideas like that." The sheriff shakes his head. "Now, how can I help you? Did some youngins' bother you? Or maybe you hit a deer up on the mountain road? If so, I need to find the right papers here. There's so many…"

The sheriff pulls some forms out of a blue folder and looks up from his seat. Recognition springs across his eyes as he notices me behind Charlie. "It's you! I knew you'd come and help me. I thought it would take you a bit longer to agree to it, but here you are." The sheriff puts one of his worn hands over his chest and tips his hat with the other one. "And I do have to apologize for saying you were a liar in the coffee shop. I knew you weren't a liar. I thought a challenge to your integrity might win you over. It's an old sheriff's trick." He winks.

I awkwardly smile. "I thought as much," I say. "I guess I am ready to help you."

The sheriff gets up and moves over to a filing cabinet. He pulls open one of the heavy, metal drawers. "Let me get the file out, and I'll brief you on the case."

Charlie clears his throat rather loudly, and the sheriff looks up. "Is that all you wanted to say, Emma? Isn't there something else you wanted to say to the gentleman?" Charlie prods.

My cheeks feel like they've been baking in an oven. I'm not exactly used to negotiating, especially with a sheriff. The two men look at me expectantly, so I take a deep breath.

"I'll help you *if* you'll help me," I say.

The sheriff seems to think about my words for a second. He nods his head slowly. "Seems fair enough. What can I do for you?"

Charlie looks at me expectantly.

"I need you to secure an interview with Davy Pinesmith for me, and if you can do that, I can look into this crime that happened."

The sheriff's round cheeks sag a bit on his face. "Now, that might be near impossible. Isn't there something else I could do?"

Before I can reply, Charlie butts in.

"Nope. Emma here doesn't budge, and she's the best of the best. She's already solved two crimes," he says pointedly.

The sheriff sits down in his chair and lets out a sigh. "If that's what I have to do to make this town safe again, then that's what I have to do."

Charlie cracks a wide smile. "I knew you were the man we thought you were. And on that point," Charlie makes himself comfortable in the seat across from the sheriff, "before you and Emma get too caught up in this murder business, I wanted to discuss the topic of cheese with you. It seems that your town is missing some."

A young waitress balances several plates on her arm as she places some biscuits and gravy in front of the sheriff and a muffin in front of me. The sheriff, Charlie, and I are in a diner in the next town over. By the time Charlie had finished launching his complaint about the lack of special cheese in the pharmacy, the sheriff announced that our conversation would have to continue over a late lunch. It turns out the sheriff hasn't missed one of his breaks in close to fifty years, and he isn't about to start now.

"I thought this would be a good place considering we're not in Sourwood, and less people will be nosing," the sheriff says to the two of us. "Anyways, let's get back to why we are here. Not too long ago, a body showed up on the property owned by the Pinesmith Boys."

"Pinesmith Boys?" Charlie asks.

"As in Davy Pinesmith?" I follow up.

The sheriff nods his head. "The same one. Him and his brother own a small farmhouse and some nice acres of land right on the south side of Goldfinch Gap, an opening right between some of the biggest mountains on the range. I reckon they might be the only ones who have land in that part of the mountains other than the state park."

The sheriff takes a small bite of his food and swallows before continuing. "Anyways, a call came in from some hikers that they had found something disturbing up on one of the trails. They were on an overlook and spotted a person not moving lower down. I went out to see, and sure enough, I found myself a bloody sight right on the south side of Goldfinch Gap, right on the property owned by the Pinesmiths." The sheriff shakes his head. "It wasn't a sight I want to dwell on too long. It's the type of thing that keeps a man up at night caught in his prayers."

The sheriff pushes his plate away. He's hardly touched any of his food.

"That's awful," I say, but I push on with the conversation. I need to keep my composure. "Have you found out anything more since discovering the body? I remember you saying that some nearby towns had helped you out at the beginning."

"We found out some things, but really not much. We identified the man who was killed, but he wasn't anyone from around here, so past that, there wasn't much to do."

As Charlie listens, his usually jolly face pales. Charlie has been around murders before, but he's never helped me solve one. I wonder if bringing him to lunch with the sheriff was a bad idea.

The sheriff doesn't seem to notice Charlie's pallor as he goes on with his story. "The man was young. His name was Ken Kitson. I was led to believe he was down this way for some recreational hiking. His friends mentioned he was active and enjoyed the outdoors. The other departments left me in the hole after that. Told me it was all some dead end, and there was no point in investigating, and that's when I reached out to you. I thought you might have some ideas for me." The sheriff leaned back and crossed his arms. "So where should we start?"

I glance at Charlie, flustered. I hadn't expected the sheriff to be so straightforward, but if I want that interview with Davy, I'll have to come up with something. A thousand ideas go through my head, but none of them seem very good. And to be honest, most of them are just from TV shows I've watched over the years, nothing a real detective would do.

The silence grows fat and thick when Charlie finally says something. "I think it's pretty obvious what we need to do," he takes a sip from his coffee and crinkles his nose. It must not be very good. "We need to get to the bottom of it."

My hope that Charlie might have been able to help me deflates.

The sheriff doesn't seem to have lost hope though, he leans forward across the table. "I can't agree more. I'll take you there."

"Where?" I ask, confused.

"To Goldfinch Gap, or as your friend here put it, to the bottom of the mountain ridge!"

Chapter Seven

MAN IN THE MOONLIGHT

In the living room of the cabin, I curl up on one of the plush, plaid recliners and flip through one of my birding guides. This part of the country is ripe with birds, and on the way back from the diner, I had managed to spot several different species that I usually don't get to see at home, one of which looked to be some sort of yellowbellied woodpecker. I can't spend too much time reading though. The sheriff told Charlie and me that he would pick us up at our cabins tomorrow bright and early to start off the investigation.

At some point, I must drift off into a dreamless sleep because when I come to, the cabin is dark, and the only thing I can see is a silver strip of moonlight coming in through the window above the round kitchen table. The digital clock in the kitchen tells me it's almost two in the morning. I force my sleepy body out of the recliner when headlights from the driveway scatter light across the cabin.

I jump in surprise and peek out the window. A car is idling in front of the cabin. Exhaust curls out of the tailgate and sends puffs of smoke into the night air. Why would someone be all the way out here at this time?

Sourwood appears to be a safe town, but maybe it isn't. After all, there was a murder not too long ago. What if someone has found out I have agreed to help the sheriff, and they have come out here to get rid of me?

Whoever is driving the car climbs out and closes the door. The moonlight outlines the silhouette of a lean man with short hair. I duck behind the curtains and hope that whoever is out there didn't see me peeking at them through the window. I look for my cellphone so that I can call Charlie, but I must've left it somewhere before I fell asleep, and I can't risk turning on the light to find it.

There's a knocking at the front door, and my mind races. It isn't smart for me to answer the door, but whoever is outside must know I'm home. My car is in the driveway, so there's no point in pretending I'm not here. Another knock rings out in the cabin, but this time, it's heavier. I really wish I had my phone so that I could call someone. The seconds tick by, and as if my thoughts have manifested, my phone vibrates. It lights up on the kitchen counter where I must've left it before I fell asleep in the old chair. I grab the phone and look at the screen. Harry is calling me.

Normally, I'd be a bit peeved about him calling me so late, especially after blowing me off, but at the moment, I can't be happier. I press answer and hold the phone up to my ear.

"Harry," I whisper, "I'm so glad you called. I think I might be in trouble. I'm staying at a cabin in the middle of nowhere, and some man has turned up at my door. I don't know what to do!"

"My advice might be a bit unconventional, but I recommend opening the door. It's freezing out here."

For a moment I'm speechless. I glance through the window again and realize that the man who got out of the car is none other than Harry!

I go and open the door for him, and he greets me with a familiar hug. I let his arms envelop me as I take in his familiar scent, and our lips draw together in a warm embrace. I know I've been a bit upset with him ever since he sent me that one-word text message, but the relief I feel now that he's here with me washes all those feelings away.

"What are you doing here? And in the middle of the night too?" I ask.

"Sorry if I scared you. I didn't mean to arrive so late, but I had car trouble. I didn't call because I had been planning on surprising you."

"The last thing I expected was for you to show up. I'm a bit embarrassed to admit it, but when I got your reply to my message, I thought you didn't really care that I couldn't hang out this weekend." I fight a blush from covering my cheeks in pink.

Harry laughs. "Yeah, I wanted to surprise you, so I couldn't say too much in my texts or else I would've given myself away. I managed to get some days off from work, so you and I can have a relaxing time in the mountains together." Harry rubs my back affectionately.

The smile that has made itself at home on my face falls.

"What's wrong?" Harry asks gently.

"I don't think this weekend will be very relaxing," I say.

I go ahead and tell Harry everything. I tell him about how the sheriff pretended to be Davy Pinesmith to get me out here and how I have agreed to help investigate the murder in exchange for an interview.

"And that's not even the strangest part," I say. "Guess who I ran into while I was in town? Charlie Kim!"

"What is he doing here?" Harry asks.

"Looking for some sort of special cheese."

Harry shakes his head. "Leave it to Charlie to end up in the mountains searching for gourmet cheese."

I spend the rest of the night catching up with Harry. Any animosity I might have felt towards him has disappeared now that I'm in his presence. I'm even a bit embarrassed that I thought he didn't care for me as much as

I care for him. He drove all the way out here just to spend some time with me. Surely, that means something.

The sun is starting to twinkle behind the mountains when we both fall into a light sleep in the recliners. I'm not sure if I have any dreams, but it feels like only seconds have ticked by before a knocking on the front door disrupts me from my stupor. The sheriff is here to take us to Goldfinch Gap.

Chapter Eight

THE SCENE AT GOLDFINCH GAP

I expect the sheriff to take us to the small farm I visited yesterday morning when I tried to interview Davy, but that isn't his plan. The sheriff parks his cruiser in a small gravel lot off of a mountain road. There are a couple other cars in the lot, but otherwise, few have decided to brave the mountain trails on the breezy day. The four of us get out of the car.

The sheriff had picked up Charlie before stopping by my cabin to grab me. He was more than happy that Harry, an actual detective, was willing to help him. (No one had the heart to tell the sheriff that Harry was a specialist detective who gathered evidence associated with peculiar cases and didn't solve murders.)

The sheriff motions for us to come near an area by the head of the trail with a map and other informational literature posted on a bulletin board behind plexiglass.

"This here is *Goldfinch Gap Trail*," he points to the map. "As we make our way up to the spot where the hikers found the body, we'll follow a trail of pink blazes. Blazes are colorful marks left on trees to help keep people on the right track so that they don't accidently go wandering into the woods."

The sheriff heads off, and we all follow. Any hesitation I felt about the sheriff's ability to navigate the trails due to his age disappears about thirty minutes into our hike. While I pause near a relatively large boulder to catch my breath with Charlie, the sheriff forges ahead. Only Harry manages to keep a close tail on him. I can see why he's still working even though he's well past retirement age. He's in amazing shape.

After another hour of trekking through the leaf littered trails, we reach an outlook that produces a spectacular view of Sourwood and the forest that surrounds it. Not far below us, I see the area that must be Goldfinch Gap. The mountain we stand on slowly rolls away towards the earth, but before meeting the mountain next to it, there is a space of relatively flat land.

"Wow," says Charlie. "Now I see why people do this hiking stuff. This view is almost as good as a five-star dinner."

Harry and I chuckle.

The sheriff takes a step out onto a large slab of limestone and points to something far out. "Do you see that small farm there?"

I go out onto the limestone rock so I can better see. It doesn't take long to find the farmhouse. Sourwood is in the distance and the main road appears as a thin, gray river surrounded by tiny boxed buildings, but there is one house that is easy to see.

"Isn't that where Davy Pinesmith lives?" I ask. "I recognize it from yesterday."

"Sure is," says the sheriff. "That line of trees at the far end of his farm marks the end of the acreage he owns with his brother. The rest of it spreads towards us until you hit that creek right over there." He points to a rivulet that slices the landscape like a dark stroke of paint.

"Anyways, the dead man, Ken Kitson, had been hit from behind. He took quite the blow. His body was found right on the other side of the creek, on the edge of the Pinesmith Boys' property," says the sheriff. "Right in the middle of Goldfinch Gap."

I take in the location the sheriff refers to with a frown. The spot where Ken Kitson was found dead would be very difficult to reach if someone tried to access it from the same public trails that we used to get up here.

"It almost looks like Kitson must've been approaching the creek from the private land and not these hiking trails," I say.

The sheriff nods in response. "I don't gather you're too far off with that assumption." He lets out a breath. "Davy isn't much help though. He says he doesn't know anything about anything, and he doesn't keep trail cams on his property." The sheriff hesitates before his next sentence. "He's also a bit difficult to get much of anything out of, as I'm sure you noticed when you met him."

"What about his brother? You said the property was owned by Davy and his brother," I say.

The sheriff shakes his head. "That's another mystery. The last time anyone around town saw Patrick Pinesmith, I had brown hair and I could touch my toes."

"You can't touch your toes?" says Charlie. He's out of breath and has arrived late to the conversation, having straggled behind us on the hike.

"I can touch my toes. I just have to bend my knees to get there," says the sheriff, rather offended. "Anyways, that's not the point. It's been a long time since Patrick stopped by Sourwood, and he's nearly impossible to speak with. He let us investigate his property and all that, but otherwise, I don't know how someone who hasn't been to Sourwood for a few decades is supposed to help us any."

The sheriff turns back to the trail. As we hike back to the car and pass the pink blazes, a stream of thoughts swims through my mind. First, we need to find out more about the man who was murdered. The little information the sheriff has managed to dig up isn't the least bit helpful. Second, not only do I need an interview with Davy for Mr. Hawking and the magazine, but now I also need to interview him about the murder.

We all climb into the cruiser, exhausted from the hike and reaching for our water bottles. The only person who seems to not be out of breath is the sheriff. Other than a small sprinkle of sweat on his forehead, no one would guess that he might have been exerting himself. Even Harry, who is in tiptop shape, has streaks of pink on his freckled cheeks.

The sheriff buckles himself in to the car. "I enjoy a light morning stroll now and again."

"Stroll," mumbles Charlie. "I seem to own a different dictionary," he huffs under his breath.

"Anyone up for breakfast?" the sheriff asks.

The sheriff drives us into town, and we park right in front of Country Time Coffee. Beatrice greets us as we enter the shop. Unlike yesterday when it was nearly empty, the shop is bustling with groups of people. In one corner, a group of gray-haired women play cards, and next to them, a large group of college-aged students are dressed for a hike. They must be stopping in for breakfast before they head out on their adventure.

Harry grabs a table for us by the window. It's actually the same one I sat at yesterday. I take a seat next to Harry and hold his hand while Charlie and the sheriff go up to the counter to order.

"There's no way we'll be able to help the sheriff. I know we've solved murders before, but those were a lot different from this. I mean, anyone in the world could've killed Ken Kitson."

Harry squeezes my hand. "I don't think we're in as much of a pickle as you think."

"You don't?"

Harry shakes his head. He looks over at the sheriff who is talking to Beatrice at the counter. "I think the reason this case doesn't have any leads is because someone is covering up tracks."

I raise my eyebrows. "You think the sheriff has something to do with the murder?"

Harry shakes his head. "No, I think he knows more than he's telling us because he's trying to protect someone."

"But who?" I ask.

Harry doesn't have time to answer because the sheriff and Charlie appear carrying a tray of freshly made sandwiches and steaming coffee.

"Ham and gouda," says Charlie. "I know the cheese isn't *the* cheese I came to Sourwood for, but the girl at the counter said it's still local."

It's quiet at our table as we eat our morning meal. I hadn't realized how hungry the hike up the mountain would make me. I don't mind the lack of conversation though. The rest of the coffee shop is chiming with noise. In fact, it's so loud that I almost don't notice when a tall man enters the shop and crosses over to the counter. Beatrice, who is passing a sandwich to one of the college-aged hikers, pales when she sees him. He orders something at the counter, and she quickly puts together a black coffee in a to-go cup and passes it to the man before he leaves the shop just as silently as he entered.

CHAPTER NINE

AROUND TOWN

"Who was that," I ask the sheriff and nod my head towards the exit where the tall man left.

The sheriff looks over his shoulder before shrugging. "I don't see anyone."

"It probably wasn't important," I mumble before taking a bite of my food.

I'm being overly suspicious. There was nothing wrong with that random man. Knowing that I need to solve a murder to get my interview is putting me on edge. I need to keep my head cool if I want to return to the office and Mr. Hawking with an interview in hand. As I glance around Country Time Coffee, an idea strikes me.

"Sheriff," I say, "I remember you saying that the man who died wasn't from Sourwood. Is that right?"

The sheriff lets out a whistle as he thinks. "Yes, that's right. Kitson was an out-of-towner."

"If this man wasn't from around here, do you think the locals might have remembered him if he visited the shops and restaurants?" I ask.

The sheriff pauses. For a second, I start to wonder if he does need hearing aids like he mentioned earlier, but then the sheriff speaks. "Now, this here is exactly why I asked you to help me. I figured he wasn't from around here, so no one would know him, but maybe we should ask around a bit."

From the corner of my eye, I see Charlie make a face of disbelief. "You haven't interviewed anyone in the town to see if they saw the victim the day of the attack? I form opinions on food for a living, and even I would know enough to do that!"

The sheriff holds his hands up in defense. "I'm a one man show. Getting a hold of that man's identity was a mountain of a task itself. If I knew what I was doing, I wouldn't have asked for help. Like I said before, I may be an experienced sheriff, but murder and Sourwood rarely mix together."

The sheriff glances at his watch. "Anyways, I figure it's about time to go. I'll head over to my office and print out a photo of the man so that we can show people around town. Maybe seeing his face will ring a bell for someone."

As the sheriff stands, one of the women playing cards in the back corner of the coffee shop bangs her fist against the table.

"Eleanor, you cheated!"

A woman in a light green cardigan wearing a string of pearls crosses her arms. She must be Eleanor. "I did no such thing, Dottie! You always act like a goose whenever you lose."

"Now ladies," the sheriff says, "this here is a fine establishment that Beatrice puts time into to make nice for all of us in town. If the card club can't be civil, you might not be allowed back." The sheriff tips his hat at the group of older women and leaves.

Dottie, the woman who had banged her fist on the table, smirks. "I'd like to see what that old man would do to our card club. He couldn't catch a murderer even if the suspect was combing the sheriff's own mustache hairs! And now, he has the guts to act like he owns the coffee shop!"

One of the other women at the table giggles, but Eleanor doesn't seem to find the comment in good manners.

"Dottie, Sheriff Melville tries his best. It must be hard running a town all by himself. Plus, you shouldn't say things like that. People will overhear and think you know something about what happened to that man up at Goldfinch Gap."

Dottie rolls her eyes. "Well, maybe I do know something about what happened at Goldfinch Gap."

"Dottie!" hisses Eleanor.

"What?" Dottie replies. "It's not like anything that goes on in this town is a secret. Now, I have to run. I have an appointment with Dr. Martinez soon. He keeps trying to say he's going to take my license away if I don't pass that silly eye exam, but every time I take it, one of those big trucks drives by the clinic because everything gets all shaky. I'll see you girls here tomorrow."

The other women at the table gather their purses and prep themselves for departure by adding rouge to their face and lipstick to their lips. They exit the coffee shop in a colorful bundle of knit sweaters.

"And I thought this little town wouldn't have any drama. This is much better than my reality TV fix." Charlie smiles mischievously. "I could watch those women all day."

Harry cracks a half smile. "I think we'll need to do more than watch, Charlie. It sounds like those ladies might be able to help us. They seem to know a lot about this town. I wouldn't mind trying to ask one or two of them a few questions."

Charlie, Harry, and I end up spending some time perusing the shops in the downtown area while the sheriff prints off the photograph he needs of Ken Kitson. Sourwood is nestled at the foot of a stretch of mountains, and Goldfinch Gap is visible right from the main road. While there aren't many businesses, the ones that are around are very unique. There's a bakery that makes sourdough loaves and chocolate chip pumpkin pie, a small library that has maybe four shelves in it, a yarn shop, and a local art gallery. My favorite shop though is Sourwood Quilts. It's probably the largest shop in town and carries beautiful handmade quilts. When we stopped inside, Charlie had to drag me away from a pink quilt with little daffodils on it that would've cost half my paycheck. While browsing around town might seem like a waste, if we have good timing, we might run into one of the card players and be able to ask her some questions.

By the time we've visited all the shops, a couple hours have gone by, so we visit the sheriff to see if he has managed to print the photograph. When we enter the office though, the sheriff isn't alone. In front of his desk, Davy Pinesmith wags a finger.

"You better do something," Davy says. His voice is rough and low. It sounds a lot different from the folk songs I listened to online, but I suppose that he recorded those decades ago.

"Davy, hold your horses," the sheriff says.

"Pretty soon I won't have any horses to hold," Davy shakes his finger again. The finger that points aggressively at the sheriff splatters something red onto the floor. "Take care of it, Melville, or you'll be wishing that you had."

Davy turns around and slightly jumps at the sight of me, Harry, and Charlie. His eyes linger a moment longer on me. I wonder if he recognizes me from when I went to his farm, but if he does, he doesn't say anything. He storms out of the office, letting the door clang behind him.

"Was Davy bleeding?" I ask. I know the sheriff probably doesn't want to talk about personal matters with us, but I had seen blood on Davy's hand when he told me to get off his property yesterday. I had assumed he had accidently cut it, but now that I've seen it bleeding twice on two separate occasions, I am not so sure.

The sheriff makes a dismissive gesture. "He cut his hand on some chicken wire when he was out working on his farm. He's redoing his whole coop. Davy is a good guy, but he complains a lot. He's mad because he thinks someone is messing with his animals. A couple hens have gone missing, and now one of his goats is gone."

"Goat stealing? I'd imagine most people would want to get rid of their smelly goat, not steal someone else's," Charlie says.

"No, nothing of that sort," replies the sheriff. "Anyways, I think it's a fox or a bear, maybe even both, taking the animals at night. We have them around here. Davy is convinced someone is trying to sabotage his farm. He thinks that a lot, but he often thinks people are after him."

"Now," says the sheriff, "should we head out and see if anyone in the town recognizes this fellow?" He holds up what must be the photo he printed of Ken Kitson. The man looks to be in his early thirties. He has thick, brown hair, a big smile, and is standing in front of a mountain wearing a hiking backpack. Based on the image alone, I would guess that he's an experienced hiker, and traversing a place like Goldfinch Gap wouldn't have been very challenging for him. It makes me wonder, why would Kitson have been on the Pinesmith's property at the bottom of Goldfinch Gap and not on the trails near the overlook?

CHAPTER TEN

CONVERSATIONS AND QUILTS

We start the search to learn more about Ken Kitson at the Country Time Coffee shop, but Beatrice claims that she hasn't seen the man before, and the group of college-aged hikers we saw earlier are not from Sourwood. If only the card players were still around, they might've had something to say.

The bakery and yarn shop are also dead ends while the gallery is only open two days a week, and today isn't one of those days. At the library, we aren't able to ask any of the patrons about the man in the photograph because the sheriff has a sneezing fit from the dusty books, and the librarian shoos him away.

After so many failures, we stop by the quilt shop where it takes all my willpower not to go and look at the pink quilt again. Now is not the time for me to buy things I don't need, especially with my job security up in the air with my failure to secure the Davy Pinesmith interview.

The shop is much quieter than it had been earlier, with only one woman sifting through tiles of fabric. Something about her green cardigan seems familiar, and when she turns around, I see that she is wearing a string of pearls. It's the woman from the coffee shop who was accused of cheating at cards, Eleanor. As the sheriff, Harry, and Charlie talk to the sales associate behind the counter, I sidle up next to her.

"Isn't that fabric beautiful?" I motion to a light blue gingham swatch that Eleanor holds in her hands.

"You think?" She asks me. "I thought it might be too busy for what I was looking for, but maybe I'll reconsider." She lets the fabric flutter back to its place on the rack while giving me a once-over. "Say, you're not from around Sourwood. Are you just stopping through?"

It appears that getting Eleanor to talk to me will be a bit easier than I thought. "I'm visiting. I'm staying in a cabin near here."

"What do you think of the town so far?" she asks.

"It's very quaint and cute. I still can't believe how beautiful the mountain backdrop is. I feel fortunate to be able to tour the town."

Eleanor seems pleased with my assessment. "Yes, yes. The town puts a lot of effort into trying to look its best for visitors. Sadly, these last few years things have been changing a bit more than I would like." Eleanor leans close to me as if worried that someone will overhear, but no one is anywhere near us. "We used to have the occasional visitor come to explore the trails, but now during the hiking season, we get big groups of hikers stopping through. There's practically no parking on the street once May hits. It's all a bit much for someone like me who is used to things going at a slower pace around here."

I try to keep myself from frowning. If what Eleanor says is true about the town being a hot spot for tourists, it may not be as easy for the locals to recall seeing Ken Kitson as Harry and I had hoped.

Before I can say anything more to Eleanor, the sheriff comes our way. When he sees her, he tips his hat. She smiles at him politely in return.

"Afternoon, Miss Eleanor. I hope you don't mind me asking, but I'm conducting a bit of an investigation." He holds up the photograph of Ken Kitson. "Do you recognize this man?"

Eleanor takes out a pair of reading glasses from her purse and looks closely at the picture. "You know, I think I do. Isn't that your grandson? His name is Marvin, right?"

"What!" The sheriff turns the photograph around so he can have a good look at it himself. He shakes his head at Eleanor. "My grandson is named *Marwin*, not *Marvin*, and he has red hair. This man's hair is dark brown."

Eleanor cringes in apology. "I say, with the way the young men wear their hair now, they all look a bit the same to me. And, you can't blame me for getting his name wrong. I was only one letter off."

The sheriff grunts. I'm hoping that he doesn't end his line of questioning here. Based on what I overheard at the coffee shop, Eleanor and her friends might know something about what happened to Ken Kitson. Thankfully, I don't have to rely on the sheriff to continue our informal interview. Harry steps up next to Eleanor and offers a handshake. She takes his hand tentatively in greeting.

"I hope you don't mind me butting in," he gives Eleanor a boyish grin that makes his nose crinkle just a little bit. "My name is Harry Starling, and I'm a detective helping Sheriff Melville with a recent crime that occurred in town."

Eleanor's face, which had taken on a bashful expression at Harry's attention, scrunches up in stress. "I was wondering when the sheriff would come around and ask me about that. I didn't know if I should come forward or not. I never know with these kinds of things what the proper thing to do is."

Harry nods at the woman kindly as she fiddles with her necklace. "Situations like this can be difficult, but we're here to listen."

"It's my friend Dottie. She keeps going around town and telling every-one that she knows something about the murder. At first, I thought it was hearsay. She does love some attention, but as time went on, she started saying things that made me wonder if she might be telling the truth."

"What kind of things?" Harry asks.

Eleanor blushes. "Oh, I really shouldn't say, but since the sheriff needs to know." Eleanor takes a deep breath. "Dottie said the night before that man was found murdered at Goldfinch Gap, someone had been lurking around the farm Davy Pinesmith lives on. According to Dottie, Davy had a fit and went out looking for the man. Apparently, Davy wasn't happy someone was on his property. He is a bit of a grouch, isn't he?"

"How would Dottie know all this?" asks the sheriff.

Eleanor's face turns from a soft pink to a bright red. "I say, this is the part I thought I shouldn't be going around and telling people. Twice a week Dottie brings dinner over to Davy, and the two of them watch the news and eat together. Both Dottie and Davy like to keep up a tough façade, but I think they've been going steady for a time now."

"Well, I'll be swarmed by bees! Who would've ever thought two such disagreeable people would agree with one another?" The sheriff shakes his head in marvel. "Anyways, you've been a great help, Eleanor. You go on with your day now."

Eleanor smiles kindly at the sheriff before scurrying away from the store.

"Ready to go for another ride in the cruiser?" asks the sheriff. "It looks like we need to stop by Dottie's house."

CHAPTER ELEVEN

THE ONLY HOUSE ON FARMER LANE

F armer Lane is a small, gravel offshoot from the main road that only has one house on it. The house itself is boxy and purple with white gables. The sheriff parks the car right on the side of the bright white porch and smooths down his uniform when he steps out.

"I should tell you three about Dottie. She has a mouth on her, so don't be surprised if she gets a bit sharp."

The sheriff climbs the stairs and opens the screen door so that he can knock. "You home, Dottie?" he calls.

In a short moment, the same woman who banged her fist on the table at the coffee shop appears in the doorway. It seems we have disturbed her from an afternoon nap. Her hair is wrapped up and she wears a fuzzy bathrobe.

"What do you want, Melville?"

The sheriff wasn't exaggerating. Dottie isn't just a tough cookie at the card table, she's tough all around.

The sheriff tips his hat. "I hope I'm not disturbing you, Dottie."

Dottie crosses her arms. "Of course you're disturbing me! I just got back from the doctor, and I was just about to lay down for my midday sleep."

The sheriff nods his head patiently. "I don't need but a moment, Dottie."

"Hurry up then! A moment is a moment too long."

"Maybe I better come in and sit down," says the sheriff.

Dottie doesn't seem to like this idea. She stands on her tiptoes and points her finger right at the sheriff's chin. "Listen, Melville, I know the laws. You're not coming in unless you're invited."

The sheriff holds his hands up. "Relax, Dottie. I'm not a vampire."

"The cat is eating. He only comes out once a day, and if I let you inside, he'll run off and won't finish his meal. Anything you need to say can be said on the porch." Dottie points to a set of rattan chairs with ratty, mouse-eaten cushions.

The five of us take a seat. Charlie looks especially put-out by the décor despite grabbing a spot in the chair that seems to be in the best condition.

"Who is that lot?" Dottie nods at me, Charlie, and Harry, speaking as if the three of us cannot hear her.

"Their helping me with the murder investigation. You know, the murder that took place up at Goldfinch Gap?"

Dottie snorts. "Of course, I've heard about Goldfinch Gap! What, do you think I never leave this house? Everyone in town knows about that murder."

"Anyways," says the sheriff, "I was hoping I could ask you some questions about what happened at Goldfinch Gap."

Dottie snorts again. "What would I know about some murder? You think I left the card club one day, went for a miles-long hike, and then shoved some man off the mountain ridge? I have a hard enough time getting out of my easy-chair to answer the door! You've really lost it, Melville."

"Now, now, Dottie. No one is accusing you of anything. I just happened to hear in town that you might have some information about what happened that night."

"Melville, you sure are getting some strange ideas!" Dottie rolls her eyes.

"I'm not here to start trouble Dottie. I'm only here to follow up on something I heard."

Despite Dottie's show of indifference, her face is slightly pink, and she doesn't reply to the sheriff's comment.

"There's a rumor going around that you were with Davy Pinesmith the night of the murder, and that while the two of you were eating dinner, he thought he saw someone out on his property, so he had a look around. Is that true, Dottie?"

Dottie stares off into the distance, refusing to meet the sheriff's eyes. "Who told you all of that? I bet it was Eleanor. She puts on the innocent act, but she sure has one big mouth!" Dottie lets out a sigh. "I suppose I have to fess up. What you heard is true."

The sheriff nods. "You've been a great help. Thanks, Dottie."

The sheriff starts to get up, but how could he possibly think the interview is over? No wonder he hasn't been able to gather any leads in the case. He hardly asks any questions.

"Dottie," Harry says before the sheriff can finish standing, "can you tell us what happened that night from your perspective?"

The sheriff nods enthusiastically. "That's a great idea! Go ahead, Dottie, tell it from your view."

Dottie begins, "I went over to Davy's house on Thursday like I always do. I don't know what lies Eleanor told you, but I bring dinner over there because Davy and I both like to watch some of the same shows. She probably made up something about us being in love, but let me tell you, I've never been in love, and I don't plan on starting now! I'm a spinster through and through." Dottie's words come out rushed, so she takes a second to catch her breath.

"Davy and I were watching one of our trivia favorites when we both heard the hens start going off. I told Davy I thought that the big, gray fox people keep spotting around town must've found a way into his coop, but Davy thought otherwise. He said he thought a person had been scoping out his property for the past few months. I shook my finger at him and told him that no one in their right mind wanted anything to do with that field of mud he calls a farm. He ignored me and went on out, looking around.

"Five minutes must've passed before Davy came running back. His face was covered with sweat, and his hands had dirt all over them. He told me that the wire around his coop had been slashed clean through!"

Harry sits forward in his seat. "Foxes don't slice through chicken wire in straight lines, only people do that."

Harry's words ring in my ear. Just before we went around town asking people about the photograph, Davy had been in the sheriff's office to complain about someone stealing his chickens and goat. Is it possible that the person who is responsible for the missing animals on Davy's farm is also somehow connected to the murder of Ken Kitson? And if so, how are the two linked?

Dottie glances at the watch on her wrist. "My show is about to start! I've missed my whole afternoon sleep too!" She huffs. "Are you done asking me these silly questions?"

"I appreciate your help, Dottie. I know it might not seem like anything, but the information you gave us might just solve a murder," the sheriff says.

Dottie dismissively waves her hand in the air at the sheriff. "Sure, sure." She lets the screen door slam behind her as she goes inside.

CHAPTER TWELVE

MATILDA PINESMITH

The sheriff drops Charlie off at his cabin rental before he takes Harry and me back to mine. He says he needs to gather all the filed reports Davy Pinesmith made in the last few weeks before he officially interviews Davy about the murder so that he doesn't miss any important clues. I have a feeling that while that may be partly true, the main reason the sheriff intends to shift through those files might have something to do with the fact that he hasn't been taking Davy's complaints seriously, and he needs to refresh his memory.

Harry and I end up spending the day in the recliners and watching the songbirds visit the feeder next to the window.

"What's that one?" Harry asks excitedly as he points to a large bird with a black body and white head. "It has a red mohawk!"

I stifle a giggle. "It's a pileated woodpecker. They love suet, which is what has attracted her to the bird feeder."

"How do you know it's a girl?"

"Do you see the markings on her face?" I point out the black stripe-like feature that stands out against the white feathers. "If she were male, she would have red there."

Harry leans back in his recliner and slowly shakes his head while grinning.

"What is so funny?" I ask.

He turns to look at me. The recliners are close enough that I can see the light freckles on his nose. "I think you're the first girlfriend that I've had that makes me excited about bird watching."

I stare back out the window at the large bird who digs around in the fresh suet. Did I just hear Harry correctly? Did he just call me his *girlfriend*? Maybe he didn't mean *girlfriend* though, maybe he just meant I was a *girl* who was his *friend*? Or maybe he didn't mean to say *girlfriend* at all, and the word just slipped.

A discreet, sideways glance at Harry makes me think whatever he meant by *girlfriend* must not have been very important. He's not even watching the birds out the window anymore. He's now fiddling with his phone.

Suddenly, he grabs my arm. "Emma, look at this!"

Harry holds up his phone for me. He's on some sort of poorly designed website that hosts local forums for Sourwood. There are various chatrooms that range in topic from church meetups to bungee jumping enthusiasts (there's even a bungee jumping church meetup forum).

"What am I looking for?" I ask.

"Don't look at the separate forums, look at the top post," Harry instructs.

I take Harry's phone and scroll up to the top of the website page. Just a few hours ago, someone with the username *sweetie_1945_rhubarbpie* posted.

sweetie_1945_rhubarbpie: **Was scrapbooking today and found some old newspaper clippings about the crime that happened in Sourwood about 60 years ago. Do people think the historical society would be interested?**

Below the *sweetie_1945_rhubarbpie* post, someone with the name *SourwoodHistorical* has posted.

SourwoodHistorical: **Bring them down to the library, and I'll take a look.**

"You interested in taking a trip to the library?" Harry asks.

Harry drives around for about ten minutes before we find a place to park near the library.

"For such a small town, it's a lot busier than I thought it would be."

"Funny, Eleanor said something similar to me at the quilt shop. She said Sourwood used to be a lot different than it is today. She said in the past few years, the tourist industry has really picked up."

"It's definitely not built for tourists. Before I found that chatroom, I had been looking for a hotel or rental for the rest of the weekend, but everything is booked up or costs my monthly paycheck. I sent Charlie a text to see if I could stay in one of the rooms in his cabin, but I haven't heard back yet." Harry ruffles his hair. He tends to do this whenever he's stressed.

When we enter the library, it's empty except for the librarian who is busy behind her desk stamping a new shipment of books. It's the smallest library I've ever visited. It's really just a large room with a handful of bookcases, two long tables, and three boxy computers.

The librarian looks up from her work and clears her throat. "May I help you?" She tilts her head to the side while speaking. She reminds me a bit of a poodle. The curly, gray hair doesn't help.

"We were wondering about the historical society. Is it located in this building?" Harry asks.

Harry's question brightens up the librarian. She flashes us a big smile. "The historical society is located just upstairs." She points to a door hidden in the corner of the room. There is a small, black plaque that says *Sourwood Historical Society* on it. "Not many tourists come and visit, but this town is more than hiking trails. It has lots of fascinating history. I'd be more than happy to show you around up there."

"That would be wonderful," I say.

She takes us up a flight of creaky, wooden steps and into a room a little bit smaller than the library downstairs. Unlike the inadequately stocked library below, this room is overflowing with shelves of books and binders with an array of filing cabinets shoved up against the wall.

"I try my best to keep it tidy, but we have so much inventory," the librarian says. "People love to donate different things they find, and I have a hard time saying no to anything."

A large poster on the wall behind the librarian catches my eye. It's a blown-up photograph of Davy Pinesmith sitting in a field and holding a guitar. Above his head are the words "Goldfinch of My Heart" in white, bubble writing.

"That's the cover art from Davy Pinesmith's hit song "Goldfinch of My Heart." He's a local. Sometimes you can spot him around town getting coffee or picking up something at the pharmacy," the librarian says.

I nod politely. I don't have the heart to tell the librarian that I've already had a couple of uncomfortable run-ins with Davy.

"If you're interested in Davy Pinesmith, we have lots of information on him. You can find it in the section towards the back of the room titled *Local Figures and People*. But there's lots of other things that might interest you. We have legal documents like land records, marriage licenses, and birth certificates that people have given us over the years. Old newspapers can be found in the blue binders on the shelves by the window. If you need anything, I'll be right downstairs."

The librarian starts to head back to the stairs, but Harry stops her. "We were actually wondering if you had anything on file about a crime that took place in Sourwood about 60 years ago?"

"You wouldn't believe it, but someone came in minutes before you did and dropped off a whole pile of newspaper clippings from right around then. What a coincidence." The librarian grabs a folder off of the table by the door. "You're more than welcome to go through it. Obviously, I haven't had the time to yet. The library is so busy these days."

I give the librarian another polite smile. I would hate to see what the library looks like on a slow day. Time must literally stop.

"Thank you so much," Harry says. "Can we go through everything at the table up here?"

"That's what it's here for," says the librarian. "If you still need more information on the Matilda Pinesmith crime, let me know."

"Matilda Pinesmith?" I ask. "As in Davy Pinesmith?"

"Yes, you were referring to the disappearance of Matilda Pinesmith, right? It's really the only significant crime that's happened in Sourwood, not counting the most recent one, that is." The librarian looks at us suspiciously and pulls the file slightly away from Harry's outstretched hand.

"Yes, that's the one we meant," I say quickly, trying to cover up my mistake. "I just didn't realize that she was related to Davy Pinesmith."

The librarian's bright smile returns to her face. "Yes, not many people realize Davy Pinesmith is from Sourwood, so I can see why you'd be surprised that Matilda Pinesmith was his sister. It's not something that was highly publicized."

She gives Harry the file.

"I'll be going now." She gives us a friendly nod and disappears down the stairs.

Harry pulls out one of the chairs at the small table and holds it out for me. "I think we have a lot of reading to do."

Chapter Thirteen

MR. HAWKING CHECKS IN

Harry and I shift through the newspaper clippings with care. While I'm in no way a seasoned, or even properly trained, detective, I do know how to look through old newspaper articles for research purposes. I have a journalism degree after all. Harry also seems right at home as he meticulously takes notes on his phone anytime he finds something of possible importance.

I spend about half-an-hour just trying to understand the basics of what happened in Sourwood 60 years ago. Apparently, Matilda Pinesmith, the older sibling of Davy and Patrick Pinesmith, disappeared one warm spring night. She had been visiting her family's farm near Goldfinch Gap and gone out for an evening walk and never returned. Her brothers, Patrick and Davy, were the last known people to see her alive.

The main suspect in the case was a young man named Finneas Ransom who had been linked to Matilda romantically. Apparently, the two had been going out for years before Matilda broke up with Finneas just a few weeks before her disappearance. Despite a lengthy investigation, nothing conclusive was ever discovered, so eventually, the case was dropped.

"Isn't this just the type of case you specialize in?" I ask Harry. "Evidence gathering for peculiar cold cases?"

Harry looks up from an article he's reading. "It does look like something that I wouldn't be surprised to come across at work, especially considering it involves a famous person like Davy Pinesmith."

Harry stares off into space.

"What's wrong?" I ask. It's not like Harry to freeze.

"Just the same thing I was thinking earlier. Why does it feel like the sheriff isn't telling us everything?" He pulls his eyebrows together in thought.

"Maybe he doesn't remember everything? Or he thinks it's not relevant?" I shrug my shoulders. "He seems a bit absentminded to me."

Harry softly drums his knuckles against the desk. "Why don't you check on the sheriff and see how he's progressing in gathering those reports Davy filed? I can stay here and sift through all these old newspapers. There's no point in both of us doing it."

I cross my arms. It looks a bit like Harry is trying to drive me off, but for what reason, I don't know. Harry isn't oblivious like the sheriff though. He picks up on my body language pretty fast.

"It's not you I don't trust. It's the sheriff. I think he might be," Harry pauses as he searches for the right word, "covering for a friend. If he's going to have any more interaction with Davy, I think one of us should be there. Those two are too close."

I'm surprised at Harry's assertion. I haven't known the sheriff long, but I consider myself a fairly good judge of character, and the sheriff seems as harmless as a church mouse. "I know you're the official detective here, Harry, but I have a hard time believing that the sheriff is covering up a murder for Davy. I mean, he emailed me to try and solve the murder. Why invite me out here if he doesn't want anyone to solve it?"

Harry shakes his head. "It's not that. I think the sheriff trusts Davy so much that the idea that Davy might be connected to any of these crimes isn't something that would occur to him. We might need to nudge him in the right direction and make sure he isn't overlooking any evidence."

Harry makes a good point. I know if I was in the sheriff's position and one of my close friends, like Charlie, had become entangled in a crime, I might not see the obvious clues.

I leave Harry reading through the information on Matilda Pinesmith and head to the sheriff's office. The sky has turned a dark gray in the time Harry and I have been in the library, and I wouldn't be surprised if it were to start raining. I wrap my sweater tighter around me as a breeze tickles my chin.

My phone buzzes in my pocket, and I step away from the sidewalk and duck under a canopy hanging over a shop window in case it starts to rain.

"Hello?" I answer.

"Emma, it's Mr. Hawking. I haven't heard from you since you left. Any updates on the Davy Pinesmith article?"

The sky above rumbles with thunder and a strong wind causes the tiny flags decorating the town's lampposts to flutter while a discarded receipt floats away down the street. I've been so worried about helping the sheriff, the article that I'm supposed to be writing has slipped my mind.

"I'm just leaving the historical society now. I talked to the woman who runs it, and she told me that the town has a whole section on Davy Pinesmith, and I'm free to use the contents." Thank goodness the librarian had randomly talked to Harry and I about Davy, or I would've had to make something up for Mr. Hawking.

"I bet they have lots of little stories that can't be found online. Nice work, Emma. I knew you'd be good for this assignment. Oh, shoot!" A commotion breaks out on Mr. Hawking's side of the line. "I have to go. I just spilt a bunch of peanuts all over the floor." He hangs up the phone. Leave it to Mr. Hawking to let a food incident interrupt his working day.

I put my phone back in my pocket and hurry along to the sheriff's office, hoping to get there before it rains. Just as I see the familiar brick façade come into view, I stop. A small crowd is gathered in front of the sheriff's office and an ambulance awaits on the curb.

CHAPTER FOURTEEN

CHARLIE'S CHARM

The ambulance pulls away and takes off down the road as small drops fall from the sky. The crowd slowly disperses. Whether from the rain or the fact that the spectacle is over, I'm not sure. Right outside the sheriff's door, I spot Beatrice. Her auburn hair is pulled back tight, and her pale skin looks a bit gray with worry.

I grab her arm, which causes her to jump.

"I'm sorry," I say. "I didn't mean to startle you, but is everything okay? I was coming from the library when I saw all the commotion."

Beatrice twists her thin lips to one side of her face. "Poor Sheriff Melville passed out. He went down right in front of me." She puts a hand to her forehead. "He was on one of his breaks, you know how he is. He never misses a break. He had just finished a cup of coffee." Beatrice's eyes grow a bit red. "He put his cup right on the counter, right in front of me, and then he went down. It was awful."

I cover the small gasp of air that escapes from my mouth. I knew the sheriff was older, but he had appeared in such good shape.

"Is he going to be okay?"

Beatrice shakes her head. "I can't tell you." She glances down at her watch. "I better head back to the shop. I'm sure word will get around fast.

Will you let me know if you hear anything?" She asks me, her eyes full of worry.

"Of course, I'll come right in and tell you if I find out anything." I give her arm a light squeeze as she heads out to her shop across the street.

I pull out my phone and send Charlie and Harry a quick text. I know Harry is busy in the library, but maybe Charlie can track down what hospital the sheriff is being taken to and check in on him. Charlie has charm and a dashing smile, so I know he'll be able to finagle information out of some unsuspecting nurse.

I try to check the sheriff's office to see if he's left anything out that could be useful, but the door is locked. As much as I would like to have a look through the Ken Kitson murder file, or even the reports that Davy has been filing, I'm not willing to risk breaking into the sheriff's office to do so, even if I know that the sheriff would be okay with it himself.

More small rain drops spatter the window on the sheriff's door. The storm is ready to begin as a cacophony of banging thunder echoes through the main street. I don't want to disturb Harry in the library, so I dash across to Country Time Coffee where Beatrice is back behind the counter making sandwiches for a group of hungry looking hikers wearing bright jackets in beachy colors like pink, orange, and blue. She seems to have recovered from the shock of the sheriff taking ill quickly, but I have a feeling she just knows how to wear a happy face when her customers demand it.

The shop is packed, so I grab a table in the back corner with only one chair. Despite the smell of fresh coffee and warm bread, the thought of food is nauseating. I've really worked myself into a tight corner. Mr. Hawking is expecting me to come back to the office in just a few days' time, but the only way I can get access to Davy Pinesmith is through the sheriff, and I don't even know where the sheriff is. Actually, much worse, I don't even know if the sheriff is okay. This last thought worries me most.

The sheriff has gone out of his way to be kind to me during my time in Sourwood, I can only hope that he'll be alright.

A loud boom of thunder shakes the walls of the coffee shop, and some of the hikers squeal and giggle. From the corner of my eye, I can see Beatrice make a face at their response as she slathers mayo onto some bread. Beatrice looks up across the counter, and her face falls to the same ashen gray it had been when the ambulance took the sheriff away. I follow her eyes to see that a rather tall man is hurrying past the coffee shop windows and headed for the pharmacy next door. In fact, it's the same man I had seen in the shop earlier in the day that had made my intuition run hot. I wander what about him spooks me so much?

Before I can think too much about him though, my phone buzzes. It's Charlie.

"Emma," Charlie's voice is smooth over the line. "I've found the hospital that they took the sheriff too. I'm outside his office right now with my car. Do you think you could meet me here?"

"I'll be out in a moment," I say. "I've been sitting in the coffee shop across from the sheriff's waiting out the rain."

It only takes a moment for me to dash outside and into Charlie's car, but just that short amount of time in the rain leaves me soaked. Charlie's car has heated seats though, so I won't stay cold for too long.

Charlie drives through the main street and out of the town of Sourwood.

"They took him to the hospital one town over, the same place where we grabbed food at that diner."

"Is the sheriff okay?"

"He'll be fine. He had a hypoglycemic episode."

"That doesn't sound good," I say. "What does that mean?"

"The sheriff is diabetic, and his sugar fell too low. They've treated him, and they'll release him soon."

I say a silent prayer in my head. I'm thankful that the sheriff will be okay. I wonder if all the excitement surrounding the murder of Ken Kitson could have somehow impacted his health. Maybe all the running around we had been doing had caused him to forget to check his glucose levels? Either way, going forward, I'm not going to let the sheriff wear himself out on my watch again.

Charlie arrives at a stoplight and rolls up behind a silver car. He drums his fingers on the steering wheel rather loudly, making it difficult for me to keep my train of thought. Charlie lets out a loud sigh.

"Are you okay?" I ask him.

"Aren't you going to ask?" he says.

"Ask what?"

Charlie lets out another sigh. "Ask me about how I figured out what hospital the sheriff went to and how I convinced the receptionist to tell me what had happened to him?"

A small smile crawls across my face, and I resist giving Charlie a playful eyeroll. I can always depend on Charlie to lighten the mood regardless of what is happening. "Charlie, how did you come by all this information?"

"I'm happy you asked, Emma, because it was no easy task." Charlie says as if he has rehearsed lines for a play. "I pretended to be the sheriff's grandson on the phone."

"And they just believed you?" I ask. Charlie's charm must come on strong over the phone.

Charlie frowns. "At first, no. The area is small, and I'm sure I sound nothing like the sheriff's grandson." Charlie leans forward and lowers his voice as if someone else is in the car. "Actually, the receptionist got a bit combative. I have a theory that her and the sheriff's grandson had some sort of falling out, but I digress."

Charlie sits back in his seat and continues. "I managed to convince the receptionist when she asked for my name."

"How'd you do that?"

"Remember when we were in that quilt shop, and that one woman said she thought the photograph of Ken Kitson looked like the sheriff's grandson? The sheriff went on about how his grandson was named *Marwin* and not *Marvin*? Well, when the receptionist asked for my name, I told her it was *Marwin*, not *Marvin*. I did it in an agitated voice as if people calling me the wrong name by one letter was the true bane of my existence. The receptionist ate it up. She believed I was Marvin! Shoot, I mean Marwin."

I let out a light chuckle. "Charlie, that's great, but what are we going to do when we show up at the hospital and the receptionist notices that you're definitely not Marwin?"

"I'm not going to claim I'm Marwin in person, that would be ridiculous!"

This time I can't help but let out a full laugh. Sometimes I think I'll never understand Charlie's logic, but somehow, he always gets what he needs with a little bit of charisma and wit, so maybe I should be trying to think more like him.

Charlie pulls the car into a well-maintained parking lot in front of a square, brick building. He finds a spot marked *visitor*, and the two of us head inside the hospital. The reception area is busy with people waiting to be seen. We wait in line behind a man who informs the receptionist that he has lost several raisins in his left ear. Out of the corner of my eye, I see Charlie trying to not laugh.

By the time it's finally our turn to talk to the receptionist, I let Charlie take the lead. I probably have a better chance of extracting the raisins from the random man's ear through sheer willpower than convincing the receptionist to let me visit the sheriff.

Charlie flashes a shiny smile and tilts his head to the side so that the lighting can highlight his salt and pepper hair. I've always found Charlie's good looks perplexing. He looks like a handsome, Golden Age of Hollywood actor who has fallen right out of the TV, but he has no interest in dating or finding love, preferring to spend his free time exploring the world in search of interesting food and dining experiences.

"I was wondering if my friend and I could drop in and see Sheriff Melville? We're close friends of his," Charlie says.

The receptionist doesn't bother to lookup from her computer. So much for Charlie's good looks. "He'll be discharged soon. You can go wait with the other visitor over there." She nods her head towards the waiting room.

I glance over to the room filled with plastic chairs and gray carpeting, but my eyes pause on a man sitting in the far corner. With his arms crossed and a sneer on his face, Davy Pinesmith is staring right at me.

Chapter Fifteen

The Hospital Visit

While Davy doesn't appear too pleased to see us, this doesn't stop Charlie from waltzing over and sitting right across from him. I follow Charlie and give Davy a weak wave. I expect him to ignore me, but surprisingly, he nods his head back.

"Happy to see we're not the only people around here who have bothered to come and check on the sheriff," Charlie says to Davy.

Davy makes a grunting sound, which I take to mean that he's heard what Charlie has to say.

"Were you in the coffee shop when the sheriff passed out?" Charlie asks. Davy curtly replies, "Nope."

It seems that not even Charlie's charm can crack Davy and his hard exterior. I'm tempted to try and engage him in conversation myself, but he doesn't seem very keen on me based on our few interactions so far, and I can't risk jeopardizing a potential interview with him. Thankfully, the three of us don't have to sit in silence for long.

The doors that lead into the clinic area of the hospital open, and the sheriff appears. He's sitting in a wheelchair being pushed by a woman with long, silver hair. She must be his wife.

"Anyways, Polly, I really think I'll be fine to walk from here," the sheriff tries to stand, but the woman that I assume to be his wife, Polly, places a firm hand on his shoulder and pushes him back into the chair.

"How am I supposed to go to work if you won't let me up out of this chair?" he asks in frustration.

Polly looks at her husband and shakes her head. "You're not going back to work for a few days. You need rest. You ended up in the hospital because you're working so much that you're not taking care of yourself!"

The sheriff crosses his arms. "That's not fair. I haven't taken a day off of work in almost twenty years, and something like this has never happened before."

Polly wags her finger in the air. "That's my point exactly. You need a break."

"You can make me sit at home, but you can't keep me from my work. I'll work from my bed."

Polly shrugs her shoulders. "Fine by me, but you're not going to leave the house for a good few days if I have anything to say about it."

Polly navigates the wheelchair to a spot away from the main hallway and takes a moment to check out at reception. Charlie and I take the opportunity to greet the sheriff. Davy does the same and shuffles behind us.

When the sheriff sees the three of us approaching, his round cheeks rise as he breaks into a smile. "Did you three come all the way down here to visit me? I'm flattered. I didn't think anyone other than my gal, Polly, cared about an old man like me."

"I'm happy you're feeling better," Charlie says. "Emma and I rushed down here as soon as we found out about what happened."

"The whole town was pretty concerned," I add. "There was a huge crowd around the ambulance when they took you away."

The sheriff's cheeks appear to pinken just a hue, but the hospital's lighting makes it difficult to know for sure. "Anyways, I'm fine. My sugar levels just went a little south a tad quicker than usual. I'm all fixed now."

Davy awkwardly shuffles in between Charlie and me. He places his hand out for the sheriff to shake. "Good that you're doing okay. See you around sheriff."

The sheriff takes Davy's hand and shakes it. "I appreciate you coming to stop in, Davy. I know you're a busy man."

Davy nods his head and leaves Charlie and I alone with the sheriff.

"He's a bit rough, but he cares," the sheriff says to us.

Neither Charlie nor I have much of a reply to that statement, so we both awkwardly nod our heads, hoping that the sheriff will change the subject soon.

Eventually, the sheriff's wife finishes up at the counter and comes over to us. "You all must be the lot of young people that my husband has been talking up to me these past few days."

Charlie flashes one of his smiles at Polly, and her eyes twinkle just the tiniest bit under the fluorescent hospital lighting. "I haven't been called a young person in almost twenty years, but I'll take the complement."

Polly giggles rather girlishly. "Well, you're certainly young compared to me and this old man," she points to the sheriff.

"Who you calling old?" the sheriff pipes up.

"You!" Polly says. "I told you we needed to get you some hearing aids!" She pats the sheriff affectionately on the shoulder. "I'm taking him home. He needs to rest," she whispers to us.

"I just rested in the hospital," the sheriff complains.

"So now you can hear me just fine? But when I ask you to help me fold the laundry you can't hear anything!" Polly crosses her arms and shakes her head.

The sheriff gives me and Charlie a conspiratorial wink that lets us know his hearing is selective on purpose.

"If you're going to make me rest at home, at least let me have some company. These young people are only in town for so long you know," the sheriff says.

"That's fine, but you'll have to chat in the living room. I'm not letting you wander around the house or sit out on the porch until you've rested." Polly pushes the sheriff towards the automatic doors that lead to the parking lot.

Charlie helps the sheriff get into his wife's car while I return the borrowed wheelchair to the emergency department. After the sheriff is buckled in, his wife gives us their address and tells us to swing on by today.

"Should we run into town and pick Harry up before we head over to their place?" I ask Charlie as we walk towards his car. "It would give Polly time to settle the sheriff in before we intrude."

"I'm alright with that," Charlie says. "You said he was still at the library, right?"

"That's where I left him, and he hasn't texted or called me, so I imagine that's where he still is."

Charlie and I get into the car. Only minutes pass before we are pulling up in front of the small library on the Sourwood main street. While we were in the hospital outside of town, the storm must've finished its tantrum. The streets are wet and unfortunate blossoms and leaves are strewn across the road like confetti. Even the bricks that line the outside of the library look dirty orange now that they've been drenched in the rain.

Charlie waits in the car as I dash inside to find Harry. I go directly up the steps to the historical area since the librarian isn't at her desk, so there's no need for small talk. When I get to the top of the staircase though, I'm greeted with an empty room. Harry must've left and forgotten to call. I'm hoping that means he found something important to the case and that's why he didn't have time to text me.

I rush back outside and tell Charlie that Harry isn't in the library.

"I think we should go on ahead to the sheriff's house," I say. "My guess is that Harry is on to something, and I don't think we should break the trail. It could be important."

Charlie nods his head. "You're the expert here. I've never solved a murder before, so I'll go with what you say."

On that note, Charlie whirls his car around and heads out to the sheriff's place.

CHAPTER SIXTEEN

THE SHERIFF EXPLAINS

T he sheriff's house stands next to a farmer's field that looks like a large, green blanket spread out at the foot of the rolling, blue mountains. The most prominent feature of the house is a wraparound porch painted in a bright white to contrast the red siding. Polly is out on the porch, rocking in a chair and knitting something long and blue. When she sees Charlie's car pull into the driveway, she waves.

"I thought you two might've gotten lost on your way over. What took so long?" Polly greets us as Charlie and I head up the steps.

"We took a detour and swung by the library to pick up a friend, but he wasn't there," I reply.

Polly's light blue eyes shine in the sunlight. Now that the storm clouds have cleared, the sun is bright above us.

"You all better come inside then," she says. "He's been restless in the hopes that you two would stop by."

The inside of the sheriff's house is clean and tidy. Like the color scheme on the outside of the house, it's painted in a variety of whites and reds. Polly shows us into a living room with white couches. Pictures decorate every centimeter of the shelves in the room. Many of them feature the sheriff out fishing or Polly at the beach with grandchildren scattered around her. They must have a big family.

On the couch nearest to the window, the sheriff is wrapped up in a checkered blanket. When he sees Charlie and I enter, he readjusts himself so that he can sit up.

"Polly was fussing about the two of you taking so long to show up here. I told her not to worry, and it looks like I was right as usual," he says. "Take a seat."

Charlie grabs a spot in a wooden chair decorated in fluffy pillows while I take a seat on the empty white couch. Polly bustles into the room with a tray of drinks and cookies. She's made some sort of homemade snickerdoodles with bits of cranberries and raisins in them. They're delicious. I thank Polly for the treats, and Charlie asks her for the recipe. Once Polly and Charlie have finished their short discussion on the advantages of raisons over dried cranberries, Polly sits down at a table in the corner of the room and busies herself with what looks to be a craft.

"Anyways," the sheriff begins, "the reason I was wanting you to come and chat outside of the hospital is because I found something odd when I was going through the reports that Davy made about all those animals, and I felt like it couldn't wait."

I sit up a bit taller on the couch and stop gnawing on my bottom lip in anticipation for what the sheriff has to say. So much has happened in such a small amount of time this afternoon that I had almost forgotten that the sheriff had been reading through those reports while Harry and I had been in the library.

"What did you find?" I ask.

"A pattern," the sheriff says. "It looks like Davy has been in my office making complaints every Saturday morning for the past couple months."

"That suggests that whoever is taking his animals isn't a fox or bear, doesn't it?" I speak my thoughts. "Foxes don't usually keep calendars when it comes to their hunting plans, and last I checked, bears don't either, so whoever is messing with the farm is probably human. Not to forget that Dottie also told us that the chicken coop had been slashed in a way that suggested human intervention as well."

"My assumption is the same," say the sheriff. "Anyways, that's not even the most peculiar part."

"The idea of a fox with a calendar is pretty peculiar to me, so this next bit must be good," Charlie grins at the sheriff, but he doesn't seem to understand the joke. Between Charlie's obsession with cheese and ill-timed humor, I'm starting to think that the sheriff might think he's missing a screw here or there.

"Davy has been filing his reports consistently every Saturday morning for two months with the exception of one Saturday." The sheriff leans towards me and away from Charlie. "And that Saturday was the Saturday that Ken Kitson was discovered dead at Goldfinch Gap."

I sit up a bit straighter in my seat. "That means that whoever is sabotaging the farm might be the same person who killed Ken Kitson. On the night that they were busy attacking Ken Kitson, maybe they didn't have time to bother with the animals."

"I thought it was a big idea," the sheriff replies with excitement.

"You two are forgetting that Davy did have his chicken coop slashed the night Kitson was murdered," Charlie says. "Dottie said so herself."

The sheriff's shoulders curve in on themselves. Charlie has deflated what little optimism had grasped the sheriff just moments ago.

"Oh, wait, I have it!" Charlie says excitedly. "It's possible that Davy didn't report anything that Saturday *because* of the murder. Maybe he was distracted with the news?" Charlie wonders. "Or maybe, Davy *is* the murderer? The reason he didn't report a missing animal that night was because he was too busy offing Ken Kitson himself!" Charlie triumphantly proclaims.

As Charlie rebuffs the sheriff's ideas, the older man's face falls. "Maybe the reports Davy were submitting weren't that important after all."

I frown. While I understand that the sheriff might be disappointed that his theory didn't pan out, I'm surprised that he doesn't seem to be able to acknowledge the possibility that his close friend could be complicit in a crime. I realize that what Harry has been saying all along is right. Maybe the sheriff is covering for his friend unintentionally. We'll never be able to figure out what happened to Ken Kitson if the sheriff doesn't open his eyes to all the possibilities. As I think about Davy, another thought crosses my mind that makes my stomach churn. If Davy does end up being the one who hurt Ken Kitson, what will Mr. Hawking say when I come back to the office with no interview and a story about how I brought down one of his favorite singers? I wish Harry was here. He'd be able to talk me down from the spiraling thoughts cascading in my mind.

"Oh shoot!" Polly says loudly from her crafting table. "I just glued the wrong photograph into my scrapbook."

"Scrapbooking!" Charlie exclaims. "How quaint!"

"Wait," I say as I think back to the message board I had read with Harry earlier in the day. "Polly, did you happen to drop off some articles about Matilda Pinesmith at the library?"

"Aren't you something!" Polly exclaims. "How'd you find out about that?"

Before I can answer, the sheriff cuts in. "What's this about Matilda Pinesmith, now?

Polly crosses her arms over her chest. "This is exactly what I'm talking about! You can't hear anything! I'm taking you to the doctor as soon as I can get you in."

The sheriff waves his hand dismissively at his wife and turns to Charlie and me. "I don't like to talk about it much, but Matilda Pinesmith happens to be the case I worked all those years ago that I was never able to solve. Up until recently, it was the darkest thing to ever happen to Sourwood."

"What happened?" Charlie asks. He hadn't been in the library with Harry and I when we met the librarian, so he doesn't have the full details like Harry and I do.

The sheriff sighs. "Matilda Pinesmith was the sister of Davy and Patrick. The three of them were thick as thieves. Patrick was the youngest at seventeen, Matilda the oldest at nineteen, and Davy right in the middle.

"At the time, Davy's career had just taken off. "Goldfinch of My Heart" was one of the top folk songs in the country, and he was getting ready to go on a tour. No one ever thought such an amazing thing would happen to someone from the small town of Sourwood, especially to someone as young as Davy."

The sheriff shakes his head back and forth slowly before resuming his tale. "The night before Davy was supposed to leave for his tour, Matilda went missing. It was Patrick who called me about it. Matilda had been at home, in the same house that Davy lives in now. Her parents retired early for the night, and Davy and Patrick stayed up later with their sister.

"When I interviewed both the boys, they claimed they had been playing guitars and singing campfire songs late into the night. It wasn't the type of thing I would've done with my sister, but they were a musical sort of family. The mother sang in the church choir and the father was known around town to bring a fiddle to weddings when asked.

"Anyways, Matilda had suggested the three of them should toast some marshmallows, so Patrick went inside the house to get the food, and Davy went off into a nearby meadow to look for some maple twigs to use as skewers. When both the boys returned, Matilda was gone.

"We had search groups, press conferences, door-to-door campaigns trying to figure out where that girl went. Anything you can think of, we did it. One of the nearby counties even did a walk with their K-9 officers through the wooded trails, but almost nothing showed up. After a while, we just had to accept that we would never know what happened to Matilda. Davy ended up going on his tour, but he was never the same after his sister disappeared. Patrick left Sourwood as soon as he graduated. I think he couldn't stand the idea of staying around in the place where Matilda had last been seen."

"It's good he left though," the sheriff's wife pipes up from her crafting table. "Patrick ended up making a big name for himself in business. Had he stayed in Sourwood, that would've never happened..."

Polly continues her monologue as she pastes photographs onto bright purple backing paper, but I have trouble paying attention. Something the sheriff said is bothering me. Like an itch on the bottom of my foot, I can't exactly figure out what is wrong, but I know something isn't right. Before I have time to come to a conclusion, Charlie is standing up from the couch and getting ready to leave.

After a few quick goodbyes, Charlie and I end up back in the car, driving on the wet roads. The earlier rain has dyed the pavement a dark black as opposed to the dusty gray I had grown accustomed to seeing in Sourwood. As Charlie takes a tight turn, a small deer runs across the road.

"That was a close one!" Charlie says with relief. "We almost got in an accident."

"Almost, but not quite," I reply.

As soon as the words leave my mouth, something clicks in my mind. *Almost*. The sheriff had said he found *almost* nothing in the woods after Matilda disappeared. That must've meant he did find something though, right?

CHAPTER SEVENTEEN

THE MESSAGE IN GRAVEL

C harlie drops me off in front of my cabin where Harry's car is still not back. Based on the low position of the sun, the day is almost over. I hope he's back soon. Whatever he found when he was researching in the library must be a hot lead.

Inside the cabin, I put the kettle on since a chill is starting to creep through the wooden walls. Tomorrow morning I'll need to stop back at the sheriff's house and ask him more about what he found when Matilda went missing. I'll also need to follow up with him about all those reports Davy filed, and while I'm at it, I might go ahead and ask the sheriff if there's any more information on Ken Kitson that he hasn't revealed. The sheriff seems to have a bad record of accidently omitting important facts. Prompting him might bring to mind some things that he thought were incidentals.

The kettle whistles like a train, breaking through my foggy thoughts. I turn the stove off before pouring the steaming water over a peppermint tea bag in a nearby mug. I'm tempted to take a sip, but I know better than to gulp down a hot drink. A low, raspy screech distracts me anyway. I could distinguish the sound anywhere. A barn owl must be nesting near the cottage. I nudge one of the cabin's windows open so that I can listen for the call a bit better. Sure enough, another screech rings out in the night like a spectral song. I wish I could catch a glimpse of the bird, but now that the sun has set, I can't see anything in the nearby woods. I could turn on the outside light, but I would risk scaring the owl away.

I tug the window back down, but stop before it's completely shut. There's another sound in the driveway, heavy steps crunching under footfalls. Could it be Harry? No, Harry would've returned with his car, and there isn't a glimpse of headlights around. It must be an animal of some sort although it sounds much too heavy to be something like a raccoon or opossum. The wooden steps that lead to the front door creak. My breath catches in my throat, and I force myself to exhale. I'm being overly paranoid. A large fox is probably just exploring the new human scents that have been left around the usually vacant rental property.

I shut the window completely and take a seat in one of the armchairs. My head has only skimmed the top of the headrest when a large crack rings out through the cottage. I spring up from the chair. It sounded as if someone had taken a sturdy branch and cracked it right against the front door.

I grab the door and thrust it open. As I do so, headlights appear on the country lane and light up a shadowy silhouette fleeing into the nearby woods. I can't make out much other than that the person appears to be wearing a hood and moving swiftly. I step out onto the stoop and a crunch comes from under my foot. I look down to see that someone, presumably the figure fleeing into the woods, has left a scattering of gravel right in front of the entrance to the cabin. My heart skips a moment when I realize that the sprinkling of stones spells a word: *LEAVE*.

CHAPTER EIGHTEEN

HARRY'S NEWS

The car that had been traveling down the country lane turns into the gravel driveway. I don't know if I should feel relief or concern. I'm happy to no longer be alone, but what if whoever is driving the car is an acquaintance of the person who ran into the woods? I don't fret long though. As the car approaches, I realize it's Harry. He pulls in behind my car and takes his time getting out. When he does finally step away from his vehicle, he heads straight for me and wraps me in a big hug, his boots disturbing the message written in gravel in the process.

"Sorry I took off like that. Something came up, and I didn't have much time. I should've sent you a text," he says.

Harry takes in my confused face. "What's wrong?"

"Did you see someone running through the woods when you drove up just now?"

Harry frowns and runs a hand through his brown hair. "No. I passed by some deer, and I think a skunk or two, but there weren't any people around." Harry looks into my eyes. His light brown ones pierce mine with arrows of curiosity. "Did something happen?"

I glance over Harry's shoulder and tug on the sleeve of his jacket. "I think we should go inside."

Harry follows me without protest. He kicks his boots off at the door and takes a seat in the same chair I had been sitting in when I first heard the owl's call.

"Someone was outside the cabin. I thought it was an animal at first, but then I heard a loud sound and went to check it out. Whoever they were, they took gravel from the driveway and rearranged it in front of the door to say *LEAVE*."

"When did all this happen?" Harry says, concern threads his brows together.

"As you were driving up to the cabin, I glimpsed them flee into the woods right when your headlights appeared."

"What did they look like?" he asks.

I shrug. "I have no idea. I just saw their shadow, and they had a hood on."

Harry shakes his head. He looks a tad bit angry. "This isn't good. I had a feeling something like this might happen, but I didn't expect it to happen so soon."

"You thought this would happen?"

"Shortly after you left the library to check on Sheriff Melville, I found something out about Matilda Pinesmith that I couldn't ignore."

I take a seat in the other armchair across from Harry and play with the loose thread on the armrest. Whatever Harry found must've been important if it had caused him to disappear for the rest of the day.

"I found the newspaper from the day Matilda disappeared."

"Did it detail her disappearance?" I ask.

"No, it was published in the morning before Matilda disappeared, so no crime would have happened yet. Apparently, the day Matilda disappeared was the same day that the local school hosted their prom night. In anticipation for the upcoming dance, the town paper published past photographs from local dances to highlight the changing fashions."

Harry is losing me. I enjoy a good fashion timeline as much as the next girl, but what does any of this have to do with Matilda's disappearance? My thoughts must appear on my face because Harry leans towards me and places a gentle hand on my knee.

"Stay with me," he says. "Everything will link up."

I nod my head to show that I'm listening once again. "So, you found a bunch of old prom photographs? Then what?"

Harry takes out his phone and shows me a photograph that he's taken of a grainy newspaper image. In the picture, a young man appears in a dark suit flanked on both sides by two teen girls dressed in prom dresses. I recognize one right away as Matilda Pinesmith. She looks exactly the same as she did in the photograph that I had seen of her and Davy standing in front of the barn. Her long hair has been pushed back in a stylish headband popular for the time period, and she wears a pink dress with a structured skirt.

"That's a photograph of Matilda with Finneas Ransom, the lead suspect in the case according to Sheriff Melville," Harry says and points to the man in the suit.

"The sheriff said they didn't find any justifiable evidence to align Ransom with the disappearance," I say. "And the sheriff already knew that Matilda and Finneas had been romantically linked, so finding an old prom picture of them together wouldn't be too surprising."

"You're absolutely right," Harry says. "My mind was running on the same track as yours when I saw this photograph, but then I looked a bit closer. Emma, look at the hands."

Harry gives me his phone and I zoom in on the hands of Matilda and Finneas. Matilda holds hers in front of her waist while Finneas's hand stays by his side.

Harry grins. "Look at the other hands," he says.

I move the zoomed in photograph over so that I can look at the hands of Finneas and the girl who stands on the other side of him. The two hands are clasped in a tight embrace, fingers entwined together.

Harry slides to the next photograph on his phone. It's another grainy photograph of the newspaper, but this time, I can see that it is the caption of the prom photo we have been so diligently studying.

Harry reads the caption aloud. "Finneas Ransom, *center*, is pictured with his long-term girlfriend, Matilda Pinesmith, *right*, and Matilda's school friend, Ella Worle, *left*, at last year's prom."

"So, Finneas is secretly holding the hand of his girlfriend's best friend?" I ask. "That's not very gentlemanly," I say as Harry puts his phone away. "I can see why the sheriff had suspected Finneas of foul play given that Matilda's relationship with him probably didn't end on a high note, but Harry, I have to be honest, I still don't understand what any of this has to do with Matilda disappearing a whole year later."

"Normally, I would agree with you, but this photo led me down a pretty deep rabbit hole." Harry turns to look me in the eyes, and a bit of moonlight catches the side of his jaw. His face betrays a seriousness I haven't seen too many times before. "Emma, I can't believe I'm saying this, but we don't have to keep conjecturing. This photo led me exactly to the source of Matilda's disappearance."

"Finneas Ransom?" I say, confused. "I suppose we could try to talk to him. I know the sheriff said his name was cleared, but if something in that photo made you believe otherwise, I guess we could give it a shot."

Harry squeezes my hand. "Unfortunately, Finneas Ransom died about twenty years ago. I was thinking maybe we could talk to Matilda."

For a short second, I think I've misheard Harry. "How can we interview someone who is a missing person?"

Harry smiles and a small twinkle touches the rim of his irises. "Emma, I may not be Sherlock Holmes when it comes to murders, but I am an expert in collecting evidence when it comes to strange and peculiar cases. Matilda tried her best to cover her tracks, but she's well and alive, and I know exactly where we can find her."

My mind buzzes with his words. Matilda is *alive*. How could that be when the sheriff was so certain something horrible had happened to her? Asking the sheriff what he did find while investigating Matilda's disappearance is now more important than ever.

"Harry, this really twists the case. I don't even know what to think. How did you find all this out?"

Harry relaxes in his chair and stretches his legs out in preparation for a long story. His head rests against the knit blanket draped over the armchair.

"I wanted to learn more about this Ella person in case she was someone that Sheriff Melville failed to follow up on back when Matilda first went missing. I called a coworker to see if she could find anything out for me on a larger database, but before I even got around to asking about Ella, a much better idea struck me. Why not ask about Matilda? So far, everything we know about her is stuff we've found in the library or things that Sheriff Melville has shared with us, but what if there's more out there that would help us understand her disappearance better? When I explained to my coworker why I wanted to find Matilda, she immediately jumped into action. Certain software that wasn't around during the decades following Matilda's disappearance are now the norm, and apparently, Matilda hasn't really been hiding at all. The problem didn't so much as lie with Matilda being stealthy, but rather, Sheriff Melville being rather unaware of newer techniques."

I inch forward onto the edge of my seat. I can tell that Harry is enjoying playing this out, but I want him to get to the details. I nod my head, encouraging him to continue the story. He sees this and smiles at me.

"I take it you want me to get to the point?" He squeezes my knee playfully. "Matilda disappeared from public record for a couple years, and then," Harry snaps his fingers, "she reappeared just like that."

"But how?" I ask.

Harry shrugs. "She wasn't a traveler and never worked in any formal capacity during the time she was missing, so she never needed to rely on official documentation. She eventually got married and legally changed her last name to her husband's, so by the time things did become more digitalized and easier to trace, she had a different name. It's a rather simple story."

I lean back in my armchair and put a hand to my forehead. "I understand how the sheriff didn't find her, but how has no one else found her? Surely, someone must have wondered where she went?"

"I think those are all things we need to find out," Harry replies. "They are also things that might be addressed if we can interview Davy and his brother, Patrick.'"

"I'm not sure about Patrick, but good luck with Davy. He's as likely to talk as a bird."

Harry laughs at my rather horrible attempt at humor. "I have a feeling he'll sing for me once he realizes what I know."

"Do you think any of this is connected to the death of Ken Kitson?"

Harry pauses for a short moment as he thinks. "I think it's definitely possible, but I'm not sure how so."

"We have a busy day tomorrow," I say. "First, we need to ask the sheriff about what he found during his investigation about Matilda. Then, we need to get Davy talking, and from there, we somehow need to get in contact with Patrick Pinesmith and Matilda."

"It's a lot to pack in," Harry says. He has deep, dark circles under his eyes and needs sleep.

"Oh, and before I forget, we also need to talk to the sheriff about those weird animal disappearances on Davy's farm. Now that I think of it, those could be connected to whoever wrote that threatening message to me in gravel rock."

Harry closes his eyes. "So much for our relaxing mountain getaway. I'll need a vacation after this trip."

CHAPTER NINETEEN

CUT FROM THE CLOTH

I meet up with Harry and Charlie at the coffee shop the following morning. After Harry and I had our conversation, he went back to Charlie's roomy cabin (Harry had wanted me to come and stay in one of the spare rooms on account of the mysterious visitor who had left the threatening gravel note, but I had refused). Thankfully, there were no more disturbing night visitors.

The three of us have nabbed a seat by the window in the busy cafe where almost every table is taken. There are some men dressed for a long ruck at the two tables next to ours, and the small group of card players, including Eleanor and Dottie, is in the far corner. I sip a bit of my warm latte as I watch the clouds outside grow gray against the morning blue sky.

"Do you think it'll storm again?" I ask.

Charlie aggressively blows on his coffee. "I hope not. This trip has been a doozy. I still don't have that cheese, and I really need it. It's the most awful thing that could've happened."

Harry raises his eyebrows, and the right side of his lips twitch in an attempt to prevent a smile.

Charlie notices this. "Other than the murder and such," he grumbles. "What have you two got on the agenda?"

Harry catches Charlie up on everything that he recently learned about Matilda. I don't think Charlie closes his gaping mouth once during the story. When Harry gets to the part about how we've decided that we'll need to interview the sheriff and all the Pinesmith siblings today, Charlie claps his hands together.

"That's perfect," he exclaims.

"What is?" Harry asks.

"Well, there's no way that the two of you are going to be able to hop around to all those places in one day. Why don't you let me interview one of them? I know I've never solved a murder like you two have, but I think I'm pretty good at squeezing details out of people." Charlie takes a sip from his drink.

Harry glances over at me, and I shrug my shoulders. "It would save us a lot of time," I add.

"I'll take Patrick Pinesmith," Charlie chimes. "I think he'll be one of the hardest people to interview since he's distanced himself so much from Sourwood, and between the three of us, I definitely have the most charisma."

"Sure," Harry replies. He tilts his head the slightest bit, and I know that he's annoyed with Charlie, but I have to agree with Charlie on this one. Between the three of us, he possesses the uncanny ability to weasel his way to information.

"I suppose Emma and I will head out to the sheriff's then," Harry says. "After that, we'll head out to Matilda. Based on what I found, she only lives about an hour from here."

Charlie shakes his head as he takes another sip of coffee.

"What?" I ask him.

"Matilda has lived for all these years, decades, in the vicinity of Sour-wood, and *no one* has noticed? I love fish as much as the next food writer, but something about this whole thing smells fishy, and not in a good way."

Before I have a chance to reply, Dottie's loud voice fills the cramped shop.

"Eleanor, you can't play that card!" she says, her face turning a bright red.

"You played the same card a few hands ago!" Eleanor pipes back.

The two men dressed with the heavy rucksacks at their feet have their eyes glued to the quarrelling scene as does a young family sitting at a table by the counter. Beatrice, who is standing behind the counter, crosses her arms and halts her sandwich making.

Harry glances down at the face of his watch. "I think we should all head out."

"I couldn't agree more," I say.

The three of us leave the shop with the gray clouds hanging low over our heads.

It's not long before Harry and I are parking the car in front of the red house that the sheriff and his wife call home. The two of them are out on the wraparound porch. The sheriff sits in a rocking chair, skimming the newspaper while Polly fiddles with a hummingbird feeder that hovers over the porch railing. When they see Harry and me pull up, they both offer friendly waves.

"We weren't expecting visitors so early this morning," Polly calls to us. "I'm still in my bathrobe and curlers! I hope you don't mind!" She consciously pokes at one of the pink contraptions that her thin hair has been wrapped around.

"Bathrobe, evening gown, it all looks the same nowadays," the sheriff jokes as Harry and I climb the stairs. "What can I do for you two?"

Polly turns around, her hands placed firmly on her hips. "You sit down. You aren't going to do anything today other than breathe and sit. You know what the doctor said." Polly turns to us with a warm smile. "I'll be right out with some coffee for the two of you. Go ahead and have a seat."

Harry and I mumble our thanks and take a seat on a wicker sofa across from the sheriff's rocking chair. The cushions on it are a dark green, and they complement the deep red of the house.

"Before you ask me anything," the sheriff begins. "I feel fine. I slept like a whale, or whatever the saying is."

"That's good to hear," I say.

"Anyways," the sheriff leans towards us on his rocking chair, "Polly will probably be in there making coffee and tidying herself up for about 15 minutes. She thinks all this talk about work is having a toll on my health, so after my visit yesterday with Emma and Charlie, she forbade me from even thinking about that murder over at Goldfinch Gap, but what she doesn't understand is it's the opposite. Not working on the case is driving me mad."

"That's what we came to talk to you about," I say in a low voice just in case Polly is hovering near one of the open windows. "When I was here yesterday, you mentioned that when you were investigating Matilda's disappearance, you found *almost* nothing, which means that you found *something*. What was it?"

An uncomfortable look crosses the sheriff's wizened face, and his eyes do a quick dart towards the front door, maybe hoping that his wife will appear and release him from having to dredge up the past with me and Harry, but no such thing occurs.

The sheriff rocks back in his chair and speaks, "When Matilda disappeared, we found some fabric that matched the clothing she was wearing that night in the woods, caught on some twigs, near Goldfinch Gap."

"Was that it?" Harry asks.

"Well, not exactly. See, we found one strip of cloth, but it wasn't like the type of thing you might normally see at the scene of a crime. It was twisted into a bunch of vegetation near the edge of a creek, and it had been torn in a straight line. Normally, when someone is in a tussle and their clothes tear, you would expect things to be a bit torn up. It was just odd."

The sheriff leans back in his chair. "It's bothered me for years. Anyways, I've always told myself it was just a coincidence, but a small part of me doesn't believe it. Sometimes I still dream about that small piece of cloth. It always appears when I'm trying to solve a puzzle or something."

Harry nods his head. "Believe it or not sheriff, you've been a big help. That perfectly cut strip of cloth you found might be more important than you realized."

The sheriff looks out onto the distant mountains. "I would like to think that."

The door to the house bangs open and Polly appears holding a tray of coffee and fruit. She no longer has curlers in her hair, and her bathrobe has been exchanged for a nice day dress that's more suitable for company.

As Polly sets the tray down, she squeals, "Oh, look at that!"

We all turn our heads to see a small, jeweled-tone hummingbird sipping nectar from the feeder nearby. The tiny bird's wings move so fast they only look light floating blurs.

"I love a good springtime hummingbird," Polly says and sighs. "I always take them to mean that some good news is on the way."

I exchange a smile with Polly, "We can only hope."

Chapter Twenty

THE MESSAGE IN BARK

Harry directs me through the winding roads as we drive pass a mix of mountain overlooks and dense forest on the way to Matilda's house. He is using a paper map because the GPS is no longer receiving any signal. Despite being off the grid, people still seem to live up in this part of the mountains. So far, we've passed at least five houses, one of which looked rather new and updated.

I take a sharp turn as the car climbs up the mountain before another quick descent appears. The road has been like this for ages, unpredictable and wild. Whenever I think we've finally hit a straight section of road, another turn appears. I press my foot against the brake pedal when the road suddenly wraps around the forest landscape like a ribbon. My car clunks loudly against a hidden pothole in the pavement.

"That didn't sound good," Harry says.

"I think I'll pull over there," I point to an arrester bed, a dirt hill next to the road designed to help runaway semis stop if they have trouble braking in the mountains.

I pull the car into the bottom area, and Harry and I get out to check the damage. Despite being in the mountains, the air smells acrid like burnt toast. We must be around some sort of odorous tree or shrub. Harry peers below my car and gives me a frown.

"Well, I don't think the pothole did us any damage, but I do think we need to rest for a bit. You must've been using the brakes a lot on the drive. They smell like they're burning up. We need to let them cool."

"Is that what that smell is?"

Harry nods his head. "You're not supposed to press down on the brake so much when going downhill."

A deep heat burns the upper part of my cheeks. "I didn't know that. I'm happy we stopped. I would've felt bad if I had lost control of the car." A catastrophic image of Harry and I flying through the trees enters my mind. It disappears though when Harry grabs my arm.

"Is that a canary?" Harry points to a bright yellow bird preening its feathers in a nearby tree. "I thought those were only found in the islands. Who would have thought we'd see one here?"

"It's a goldfinch. I figured there was probably a healthy population in this area considering the name of Goldfinch Gap. They're beautiful birds to see in person," I reply.

"Well, at least I got your mind off the car for a moment there," he says before unleashing a grin on me. Sometimes I wonder if Harry can read my thoughts.

The bright yellow bird does look like a canary except for the dark feathers on its wings and the dark cap on its head. Another bird joins the preening one and settles on the tree branch above the car. The yellow on this bird is a tad different, slightly olive-colored.

"It looks like his mate has arrived. Maybe they have a nest nearby," I say.

Harry and I watch the birds for bit as they hop around the tree limbs, and the male sings a song. Harry wraps his arm around my back and gives me a soft kiss along the side of my head. During moments like this I can't help but wonder what this weekend might've been like had the sheriff not called me down to Sourwood. Would Harry and I be officially dating now? Harry had called me his girlfriend, but I still don't know if that was a slip of the tongue or not.

Eventually, the two birds disappear into thicker vegetation, and Harry and I go back to the car. I notice right away that the unpleasant smell that had permeated my nostrils has now disappeared in favor of the scent of wet leaves and damp wood.

"I'll try to be better about riding the brakes this time," I say to Harry as we buckle ourselves in.

Before I pull back onto the road, an older, green car passes by slowly. For a moment, I think I recognize the man behind the wheel, but that can't be right. Other than the sheriff or maybe Davy, there's not one man around here I should recognize. I put the car in drive and continue on my way. Despite hoping that the worst of the drive is over, the road ends up becoming even more steep and curvy. I make a mental note to not live in the deep mountains. There's no way I could drive these roads on a daily basis.

Finally, the road levels out, and we cruise through flat fields where the sharp mountains are only a backdrop behind Harry and I. Matilda must live on the other side of the mountain range from Sourwood. After driving through a blink-town with only a gas station and vet clinic, Harry instructs me to slow the car and turn into a short driveway in front of a tiny, white house with a garden filled with pink and purple flowers. Near the front door, a group of garden gnomes with green hats is arranged in a circle as if they have important business to discuss.

Harry and I stride up to the door and ring the doorbell. A light chime plays, and the two of us wait to see if anyone comes by. The sound of bees buzzing near the flowers and a squirrel gnawing on bark are the only noises I hear. Maybe Matilda has gone out for the day? I hope it's for a quick lunch and not something longer like a day trip.

"What should we do?" I finally speak when it seems for certain no one is going to appear at the door.

Harry places his hands on his hips and dips his head in thought. He hadn't been expecting a no-show at Matilda's house.

"There's not really anywhere for us to go if we wanted to wait for her to return," I say. "There was hardly anything in that town we drove through."

Harry ruffles is hair. "Is there another town past this one? Maybe there's a diner or something closer than we think."

I pull out my phone to check, but there's no service. I'm not exactly inclined to go searching out the next mountain town either. For all I know, there will be even less things there than there are here. Harry and I head back to the car. We make a short stop and fill my gas tank up since the price here is cheaper than it is in Sourwood.

"Let's check back once more. Maybe she's back from whatever errand she was running," Harry suggests once we're both buckled back in the car.

As we approach Matilda's colorful garden a second time, the front door opens, and a tall man in all black exists the house. He runs to a green car parked by the garden gnomes. He's only in the car for a second before it is started up and pulling away from the driveway. I tap the gas in the hopes of catching up, but the car is already disappearing around a corner down the road.

"Are we following the car?" Harry asks, confused.

"Doesn't it look like the one that drove by us on the mountain?"

"Possibly, but I don't think that's relative to the case. Remember, we just want to interview Matilda."

I slow the car and give Harry a short nod. I know he's right, but for some reason, the man who ran into the car reminds me of someone I knew. I turn the car around and drive back to Matilda's house and park, but soon large drops of rain flatten themselves against the windshield. I hope it's just a passing shower. I can't imagine driving through the mountains again with the added weather of rain and wind. We both hop out of the car for the second time and hurry to Matilda's front door where Harry rings the doorbell again.

We stand waiting, the plops of rain creating cold taps on our heads. Finally, a light flickers on inside the house, and the white, lacy curtains flutter. Harry and I shift our feet, expecting the door to open at any moment, but once again, nothing happens. New movement in the window catches my eye, but it's only an orange cat.

"She probably has those sensor lights that turn on whenever they detect motion. I bet the cat set them off," Harry says while pointing to the feline in the window.

An abnormally large raindrop lands on the tip of my nose. My clothing is damper than I realized, and my socks feel squishy in my shoes.

"I think we should go," I say. "Maybe we should call back another time."

Harry doesn't argue. We settle back into the car, and I reverse out of the driveway. Before accelerating down the road, I give Matilda's house one more look. The curtains flutter closed as the orange cat disappears behind them, but I could swear that for a minute, I saw the face of Davy Pinesmith peeking out at me.

By the time we get back to my cabin and have cell service, I have two missed calls on my phone, one from my mother and one from Mr. Hawking. I call both of them back, but neither picks up to my relief. I'm not in a chatty mood for my mother nor am I in the mood to dodge the questions that Mr. Hawking will surely have for me about Davy.

As I place my phone down on the countertop, Harry's stomach lets out an audible rumble.

"Sorry about that," he says as pink blushes his fair cheeks. "My stomach doesn't seem to be aware that I'm in the middle of a murder investigation."

"Want to grab some food in town? I wouldn't mind some myself."

The two of us put on our boots and trudge out to the car.

"What's that?" Harry points to something white stuck to my windshield.

"It's just some bark from that birch tree," I say while gesturing to the white tree whose limbs hover over my car. "I found some on my windshield when I first got here."

I go ahead and slip into the driver's seat of the car while Harry grabs the birch bark from the windshield. Instead of tossing it onto the ground though, Harry brings it into the car with him and furrows his brows.

"It's birch bark alright, but someone has used it as paper."

He holds the thin, white bark up so that I can see it better. Harry is right. Someone has written what looks like the words *STOP LOOKING* in small font on the bottom of the paper-like bark. I grasp the rough material with my hand and trace my finger over the writing just to make sure it really is there. It is.

"Do you think that there might've been a note written on the birch bark I found on my windshield that first time?" I ask Harry uneasily.

Harry runs a hand through his hair. "It's possible, but regardless, someone has now left at least two threatening notes for you."

"Or us," I correct. "Whoever left this note would've had to do so right after they saw us get out of the car and into the cabin."

Harry nods his head slowly. "Do you think Charlie has food at his cabin?"

I tilt my head to the side at the sudden change in subject. "Charlie will definitely have food at his cabin. He's Charlie, and he loves food, but what does that have to do with someone leaving us threatening notes?"

"I'm just thinking that if someone is sending us these notes because we're snooping around the Matilda Pinesmith and Ken Kitson cases, there is a probability that someone is leaving him notes too, and it wouldn't be a bad idea for us to go checkout his cabin and see," Harry replies.

"That makes sense," I say. "But the food part? I'm still not following. I have food here if you need some right at this very moment."

Harry's stomach lets out a loud grumble that sounds more like a turkey than something produced from the human anatomy.

I stifle a giggle.

"Kill two birds with one stone?" He looks up at me innocently while trying to hide his smile, but nothing he can do can stop the small dimple he gets on his cheek from appearing. "I figure we could look for clues and eat a sandwich at the same time."

I put the car into drive. "Who am I to keep a man from his sandwich?"

Harry finally lets his smile dash across his face, and the two of us make our way to Charlie's rental.

Chapter Twenty-One
BAD NEWS

The outside of Charlie's cabin is picturesque. The large cabin stretches towards the wooded sky with its long, reflective windows. Somewhere in the woods, the sharp call of a blue jay penetrates the otherwise quiet mountain forest.

The only car in the driveway other than mine is Harry's since he has been staying with Charlie, but there's no sign of a mysterious note left on his windshield like there was on mine. Harry and I crunch up the gravel walk in our boots and up the steps of the intricate deck, painted black to match the siding of the cabin. The glass door to the cabin has an electronic lock barring entry from strangers. Harry taps in a code, and a metallic click signals that we can enter. Inside, the cabin's dark exterior transforms into light grays and whites. I'm still amazed at the design of the structure.

"Where should we look first?" I ask Harry. "Actually, what are we even looking for?"

"I would say a letter or something arranged to make a word. Both warnings you received were written out, so I'm assuming that whoever left them is going to keep using the same style."

I look around the cavernous living room with its cathedral-like ceiling and high windows that lead to the outside world. "With the same logic, I suppose we should be searching around the outside of the property. Both of the notes left at my cabin were outside."

"Sounds like a plan," Harrys says. "Let me grab something from my room upstairs, and I'll meet you there."

Harry disappears down a hallway off of the kitchen, and I let myself back onto the porch. The first thing I do is check the deck for words that have been spelled out in gravel like at my cabin, but the deck is swept clean of debris. Not even a crinkly leaf is to be seen.

I step off the deck and make my way around the outside of the house in case something has been posted on a window or nearby another entrance. I take special care to avoid three-leaf plants, reminding myself that I don't need a poison-ivy rash on top of a failed interview and a murder investigation. I find nothing except a persnickety black squirrel eating a rather large acorn. I inform the creature that he's being unnecessarily noisy because I could hear him rustling and crunching the whole time that I was scoping out the property.

I round the front of the house, and find Harry bent over the tires of his car. He shakes his head and presses a freckled hand to his forehead.

"What's wrong?" I jog towards him. Did he find something that we had missed earlier when walking up the driveway?

"Someone has slashed my back tires!" He points to the deflated rubber.

I bend down to inspect Harry's wheels. "How could that have happened? When we were inside, we would've seen someone through the windows, but we didn't."

Harry shrugs his shoulders in defeat. "And when you were outside, you definitely would've heard something."

"All I came across was a squirrel," I reply. "Although, now that I think about it, the squirrel was being rather loud." I cross my arms in frustration. "I bet all that rustling and crunching I heard wasn't just the squirrel. I can't believe whoever has been doing these things was right under our noses, and I missed it."

"It's not your fault," Harry says. The sparks in his eyes tell me that he's still upset at his tires being destroyed, but not an ounce of that is directed at me. "Whoever is following us has a better idea of this area than we do. Maybe they were hiding out in the woods for us when we got here. We have no idea. We just need to be careful."

Harry and I go back inside and busy ourselves as we wait to hear back from Charlie. Maybe he had a more successful day than we did in terms of tracking down information about the case. All Harry and I have managed to do is go to an empty house, be left a threatening note, and get some tires slashed. Not much to show for a morning of sleuthing.

Harry puts together a cold cut sandwich in the kitchen while I daydream out the windows of the cabin, willing for the person who has been leaving us notes to materialize from the woods. Of course, no such thing happens. I'm so distraught over Harry's tires that I can't even appreciate the bird-watching from Charlie's cabin. Not even a cedar waxwing with a bright yellow tipped tail eating berries from a flowering tree gets me excited.

Harry passes me a sandwich and joins me in the living room. He takes a big bite of his lunch. He must be starving.

"I called Charlie, but there was no answer." Harry takes a sip of water before taking another giant bite of his sandwich.

"He's probably busy putting on the charm to get as much information out of Patrick Pinesmith as he can. I imagine by the time he comes back, he'll have solved the whole murder of Ken Kitson," I grumble before taking a small piece of my own sandwich. I find it hard to eat when everything seems to be going so wrong.

As if in answer to our questions, Charlie's car appears at the bottom of the steep driveway. He pulls behind my own car and gets out. The first thing I notice is that he doesn't look like himself. His lips are taut with a frown, and he has gray circles under his usually bright eyes.

Harry sets his empty plate down on the coffee table and opens the door for Charlie. Upon entering, Charlie kicks off his shoes before dramatically flopping into one of the dark leather chairs in the living room.

"Please tell me that the two of you had a wonderful outing with Miss Matilda Pinesmith. I don't think I can take any more bad news." Charlie lets out a sigh.

Harry and I exchange a look. I don't think we've ever seen Charlie without his luster.

"No one was at home when we stopped by," Harry says.

"And someone slashed Harry's tires, so it wasn't the best day," I reply before nibbling at my sandwich.

Charlie rubs his temples. "To think that when I left my house just a few days ago, I thought I would be on my way to pick up some nice cheese from the little town of Sourwood, but alas, the world seems to laugh cruelly at me."

"What happened?" Harry breaks into Charlie's monologue. "Did the meeting with Patrick not go well?"

"No, it did not," Charlie says. "It didn't go well because it never happened at all."

"Sounds like he's a bit like his brother then," I murmur while placing my plate with its barely touched sandwich on the end table. "Trying to get Davy to talk is like trying to get a cat to sing or a bird to meow. I'm not surprised his brother Patrick is just as unwilling."

"It's not that," Charlie says.

"What is it then?" Harry leans forward on his seat.

Charlie's black eyes stare off into the forest landscape outside the window where a small chickadee flashes in between the trees.

Charlie shakes his head slowly. "Patrick Pinesmith is dead."

Chapter Twenty-Two

THE FALL OF CHARLIE

"Dead?" Harry stands up. "When? How?"

Charlie flops his legs over the side of his chair in a way rather unbecoming for a gentleman. "I don't know. It was horrifyingly embarrassing."

"Why?" I ask. "Did Patrick die in the presence of a forbidden lover or something?"

Charlie lets his head lay limply against one of the chair's armrests. "No, I was embarrassed, not Patrick. Patrick died from an illness he had been struggling with for some time. Unlike me, who died from embarrassment at my faux-pas. I'll never be able to show my face in public again."

Harry and I exchange frowns. I get up and cross the room to give Charlie a friendly pat on the shoulder.

"I'm sure whatever happened wasn't that bad," I say.

Charlie looks up at me, and I'm surprised to see that his dark eyes are watery with tears.

"Tell us what happened," I perch on the edge of his armrest.

Charlie closes his eyes and reverts to rubbing his temples again. "I visited the house at the address you gave me, Harry. It was a couple hours from Sourwood, but I didn't mind because it gave me lots of time to think about how I would introduce myself to Patrick Pinesmith and get him to talk to me.

"Eventually, I came up with the idea that I would be an old pal who was in town on some food related errand. Not the most creative story, but one that wouldn't elicit too many questions, or so I thought. When I get to Patrick's house, a lovely brick colonial I might add, there are quite a few cars coming out of the driveway. I don't think much of it. Maybe Patrick hosts a book club or something similar?

"I ring the doorbell, and right away, it's answered by a woman wearing a demure, floor-length dress. Confident me doesn't wait for her to welcome me or invite me inside. No, I have to have complete faith in my Charlie charisma that I make the first move.

"I tell her that Patrick and I met a few months ago at a party, and that he had invited me to stop by his house if I ever was in town. I go on to tell her about how I'm a food writer and about how Patrick and I bonded over a chocolate strawberry pie at this party for our mutual friend.

"At this point, I'm blathering on while standing at the front door of this random house when the lady finally interrupts me. Do you know what she says to me?"

Charlie pauses his story and looks between Harry and I as if we might know what the answer to his question is. The two of us remain silent long enough for Charlie to continue his story.

"This woman looks me right in the eyes, and she says: *Patrick Pinesmith is dead*. She is cleaning up after the funeral reception. She starts to close the door, but before she closes it all the way, she stops, looks me right in the eye again and says: *And Patrick was allergic to strawberries and hated chocolate. Also, he hadn't left his house in twenty years.*"

Charlie takes a long breath. "Then, she closes the door, but that's not the worst part. After she closes the door, I hear her *lock it.*" Charlie hangs his head low. "I've never been so embarrassed in my life."

I give Charlie another gentle pat on the back. "It's okay, Charlie. You'll probably never see that woman ever again."

Harry gives Charlie a warm smile. "And you did exactly what you needed to do. You went and found out information about Patrick Pinesmith for us. It wasn't exactly the information we thought we would find out, but it was information none the less."

Charlie pulls himself out of the chair. "I hope you two don't mind, but I'm going to go take a rest in my room. I hope that woman doesn't have any important connections to the food industry, or people will think I'm off my rocker."

Charlie slowly trudges up the stairs.

Once he's out of earshot, I turn to Harry.

"Poor Charlie," I say quietly.

Harry doesn't reply. His eyes have narrowed, and he's drumming his fingers on his knees.

"What's wrong?" I ask Harry.

"Do you think it was possible for someone at that funeral to have gone to the service, the reception, and then had time to show up at your cabin and leave a note on your car and slash my tires?" he asks me.

"I suppose that would depend on how long the woman at the door had been cleaning up the reception." I think back to Charlie's story. "When Charlie showed up, the reception must've just ended. Remember, he said a bunch of cars were coming out of Patrick's driveway."

"We need to figure out who went to the reception. It could help us narrow down our suspect list as to who is leaving you notes and possibly even help us figure out who murdered Ken Kitson."

I absent-mindedly trace a circle on my leg. "How are we supposed to find out who was in attendance?"

"We'll need to ask someone who was there, like a sibling," Harry give me a weary glance, and I know exactly what that look means. We're either going to have to get Davy to talk to us, or head back out to Matilda's house and hope she will.

CHAPTER TWENTY-THREE

THE STRANGER IN THE FIELD

A cold front must be on the move because the small glimpses of spring that had been present in the mountains have all disappeared to be replaced by a nasty wind. I sip from a mug of hot chocolate as I gaze out the windows in Charlie's cabin and watch the blossoms swirl in the air. Harry and I have spent that last hour trying to come up with ways to convince Davy to talk to us about Patrick or Matilda, but nothing notable has come to mind, leaving driving back to Matilda's house tomorrow as our only option.

"Do you think Charlie will be okay?" I ask Harry who sits across from me. "He's been up in his room for almost an hour."

Harry glances at his watch before letting his eyes linger on the stairs. "He might be napping. He had a longer drive than us after all," he says.

My cellphone buzzes in my pocket. It's a text from Mr. Hawking asking me how everything is going. The small amount of food I managed to eat at lunch does a flip in my stomach as I'm washed in guilt. I have done absolutely nothing when it comes to writing my article for Mr. Hawking.

I can't even fathom coming up with something to say to him to buy me more time.

Harry picks up on the tension. "What's wrong?" he asks.

I watch a pink petal get picked up by the wind before gently bounding towards the mossy ground. "Mr. Hawking texted again. I don't know what to do. He might fire me if he finds out that the sheriff was the one who baited me to come down here by pretending to be Davy Pinesmith."

"Why don't we head back to the library? At the least you can gather some information about Davy to use in your article."

I concede to Harry's point. We bundle up and head out to my car. We'll be taking mine since Harry's will be out of commission for a little while. He's already gone ahead and sent an email to his insurance about the slashed tires, but he has yet to hear anything back.

When we get to the main street of Sourwood, it is devoid of cars and pedestrians. The usual groups of hikers are gone, and no locals peruse the shop windows. Has something happened within the time we ate breakfast at the coffee shop and now?

I pull into a parking spot in front of Country Time Coffee, and Harry and I get out. A small sign on the door indicates that it closed early today. Harry and I continue down the sidewalk towards the library. On our way, we see that the bakery has its lights turned off, and the yarn shop's open sign has been turned off as well.

"Is it a holiday?" I peer inside *Sourwood Quilts*, but no one is around.

By the time we get to the doors of the library, I'm half expecting it to be shut and locked, but to my surprise, the door is cracked open, and the librarian is behind her desk. A large book is sprawled out in front of her.

"You two are back," she absently pats at her curly, gray tresses. "Is there anything I can help you with?"

Harry leans on the counter. "Yes, but it's not exactly library related."

This interests the librarian. She raises her thin eyebrows. "Ask away," she says.

"Is there a reason why all the shops are closed?"

The librarian makes a dismissive gesture with her hand. "There is a reason, but not a *good* reason." She shifts her eyes around as if to make sure no one in the library is about to hear what she is going to say, but Harry and I are the only other people present. "It's the weather. Whenever they say we're going to get a set of bad storms, every shop on the street closes up."

"Does it flood in Sourwood or something?" I can't imagine why every shop owner would close their doors just because of a small chance of a thunderstorm.

The librarian chuckles at my question. "Sourwood has never had any flooding, at least not while I've been here. We're too far up the mountains. I should correct myself though, not every shop closes. The bakery is open rain or shine until about one, so if it's closed up right now, that's just normal business hours. The other shops though, if they're dark for the day, it's because Beatrice doesn't like bad storms."

"Beatrice, as in Beatrice from Country Time Coffee?" I ask.

The librarian nods her head. "That's the one. She owns the coffee shop, the yarn shop, the quilt shop, and the art gallery. Oh, and the pharmacy. She owns almost all of Sourwood. Good thing too. She's a mighty smart business woman."

I'm a bit embarrassed to admit that quiet Beatrice isn't exactly who I imagine when I think about a business mogul, but she does run a tight ship at the coffee shop, so it makes sense for her to be successful when it comes to other enterprises.

"We had a small storm yesterday though, and the coffee shop was still open then," Harry says.

The librarian shrugs her shoulders. "Once in a while Beatrice will change her mind and stay open during some rough rains, especially if she thinks it's bound to be a busy business day, but that only happens once in a blue moon, and definitely not multiple days in a row."

Switching subjects, Harry asks the librarian if we are free to use the upstairs rooms to do some research.

The librarian smiles and nods. "Anytime! That's what we're here for. I'll be at the desk if you need anything."

The librarian goes back to her oversized book, and Harry and I climb the squeaky stairs that lead to the historical society room. Other than an odd whistling sound coming from one of the windows every time the wind pushes against it, the room is exactly how we left it. Harry goes over to the section where he had previously found information about Davy.

"What type of information would help with your writing?" he asks me.

"It should be stuff related to his song "Goldfinch of My Heart" since that will be the focus of the article. Even things like dates when the song was released or if Davy played any local shows can add background to the piece."

Harry and I examine old newspapers, photographs, and even two old yearbooks. I manage to gather some good background information like how Davy was discovered at a young age, how his most famous song found popularity on the charts, and how he toured across the country for fifteen years and released five albums before cashing in on an early retirement and retreating to his Sourwood home to take over his parents' farm. It's a successful afternoon, and the previous gnawing guilt I had felt for abandoning Mr. Hawking's article has abated.

At the sound of heavy thunder that reminds me more of a train than something nature-made, Harry and I tidy the room back up and head out. As we walk down the deserted sidewalk, I notice someone loitering outside of the sheriff's office, a small woman pacing back and forth. It's Eleanor. She's wearing a soft blue pencil skirt with a matching sweater and is pulling at the string of pearls around her neck. She sees us as we near, and she rushes over.

"I say, I'm so thankful that the two of you showed up here!" Eleanor cries. "I knew the sheriff had taken ill, but I was hoping that someone would stop by his office because I had to tell him the most urgent thing. I suppose you two could give him the message? I'd drive up to his house, but I don't know if Polly is letting visitors see him yet."

"Of course, we would be happy to help," Harry steps forward.

Eleanor loosens her hold around her pearl necklace, and her white knuckles regain some of their color.

"Dottie and I were on our way home from playing cards. We had been hoping to spend most of the day at the coffee shop, but Beatrice doesn't like storms, so she closed up early. Dottie decided to head over to her *friend's* house," Eleanor whispers the word friend and gives us a pointed look.

"You mean Davy Pinesmith?" I ask.

Eleanor's face pales and she gives me a quick, affirming nod before looking around the street as if someone might be waiting to pounce on her if she even hints that Dottie and Davy know each other's first names.

"When I got home, my phone was ringing like it was a holiday. It was Dottie. She said that she had driven over to *his* house, and when she got over there, she saw a strange man out in one of the fields. She said she had never seen the man before in her life. I asked her if it was possibly a hiker who had wandered off the trail, but she said he was dressed in a suit!"

"Did Dottie run home right away to call you as soon as she saw the strange man?" Harry asks.

Eleanor's thin hands return to grasping her pearl necklace. "You would think she would have been sensible enough to do that, but she didn't!

She told me she went up to Davy's front door and banged on it to see if Davy knew that someone was out in his field. No one answered. She went around the back of the house and found a green car parked near the field. That was when the man in the field spotted her! She said she just about wet her pants when she realized he was heading her way! Dottie is fast though. Back when we were in school, she was captain of the field hockey team. She took off for her own car, and the man never caught up to her, but she called me as soon as she got home."

"Thank goodness she's alright," I say.

Dottie could have been seriously hurt had the stranger managed to catch up with her, but why would a man be wandering around in Davy's farm field in the first place? Not only that, but *who* could have been wandering around it. It couldn't have been Davy, Dottie would've recognized him if it was.

"She didn't want me to tell anyone," Eleanor leans close to us. "She doesn't want it getting around town that she was over at Davy's house, but I think someone needs to go over there and make sure that this man didn't do something bad on Davy's property."

"You did the right thing by telling us, Eleanor," Harry says. "I know the sheriff isn't well right now, but Emma and I can go over to Davy's farm and make sure everything is alright. Sheriff Melville entrusted us to help him while he's recovering, so we're up for the job."

After Eleanor thanks us and leaves us her phone number so that we can call her when we're done checking in on Davy's farm, Harry sees that she gets to her car okay. Once she's out of view, I turn to Harry.

"When I first saw Sourwood, I thought I would be enjoying a nice getaway to a scenic mountain town. I never knew I could be so wrong," I say.

"That makes two of us," Harry says.

CHAPTER TWENTY-FOUR
CRACKED EGGS

D avy's farm appears exactly like it did when I visited the other day. The rickety barn looks like it will fall over at any moment, and the paint on the house is still peeling. Harry and I peer around the back of the house where Eleanor says Dottie saw the car, but all that is there is an empty field with a few trees and the occasional goldfinch dashing across the air.

"It all looks okay to me," Harry says. "I didn't see any broken windows or doors that had been forced open, so I don't think there was a robbery or a break-in"

I take a few steps into the field and find light tire tracks in the damp dirt. Near the tracks, a ripped paper is on the ground. I pick it up and unfold it to see that it's a funeral program for Patrick Pinesmith.

"Even if there's no evidence someone was trying to get into the house, it's obvious that someone was in the field," I say.

"But why would someone be traipsing around the field?" Harry asks.

I pass the pamphlet to him so that he can get a better look at it. "I'm not sure why, but I think I know who," I say.

"You do?"

I look into Harry's light amber eyes. "The same man who drove by us in the mountains in the green car, and the same tall man that was parked outside Matilda's house, also in a green car."

"The same car you tried to follow?" Harry asks.

"That's the one," I reply.

The sound of wheels running over gravel interrupts us. Someone is approaching the farmhouse. Harry and I peek around the house and see a light blue truck pulling into the driveway. Harry attempts to move out into the open, but I grab him before he's able to reveal himself.

"What's wrong?" he asks. "It's just Davy."

"Exactly," I say. "It's Davy. Last time I showed up here and tried to get an interview from him he wasn't the best example of friendly. If he finds out I've come back, I might never get that interview for the magazine."

Harry frowns at me. "Emma, your car is already parked in the driveway. I don't know much about Davy, but I imagine he'll notice a random car in his driveway. There's no point in hiding from him." Harry picks up my hand and gives it a light squeeze. "In fact, I bet Davy would be happy to learn that we came over here to make sure everything was okay after someone was sneaking around his property."

I understand Harry's perspective, but I'm not sure that he grasps mine. If I make Davy upset like I did the first time I approached him, I don't think any amount of sleuthing will get me an interview with him, and I need that interview. Mr. Hawking already struggles to remember my name. The last thing I need is for him to know exactly who I am because I messed up so bad.

In the end, it's not my decision. The back door of Davy's house swings open, and the grizzly man himself appears. Davy has fire in his eyes as he stares at the two of us huddled by his back window.

"Hello," Harry steps forward. "Emma and I here were in town when someone told us that a suspicious person—"

Before Harry can finish, Davy storms over to us. "I don't give a flying hoot what you're doing on my land. I'm just happy you're here."

"You are?" I'm in shock.

"I don't have time for niceties or chatty chats. I've had a rough day, and I need your help." Davy takes off for his lopsided barn.

Harry and I practically jog after him as his long legs stride along a well-worn path in the grass. Behind the barn, a chicken coop is constructed next to a gray goat house. When the animals see Davy come around the corner, they bleat and cluck. Despite his rough nature with humans, he must have a gentle disposition with animals as they take to him quickly.

Davy opens the door to the coop, and several chickens rush out onto the lawn. "Don't worry about Hariet and Henrietta." He motions to two fat, brown hens. "They're proper ladies who don't like to stray too far from home. Now Heloise," he points to a hen with white feathers and a mean looking face, "she's bound to get killed by a fox if she doesn't stop wandering over to the woods." As if on cue, the chicken starts to peck her way over to the tree line.

Davy motions for Harry and I to follow him around to the back section of the coop where there are wooden slats protecting the chickens from outside predators. "While I was out today somebody snuck onto my land and pulled another fast one on me. Look at the mess they left. Tell the sheriff that a bear did that!" Davy points to the wooden fencing.

On the grass lay a mosaic of broken egg shells from where they fell after being smashed against the back of the coop. Someone has egged Davy's hen enclosure!

"Did you just discover this?" Harry asks. He uses his foot to shift the cracked shells around on the ground to see if there's anything under them.

"I had an, erm, errand to run today." Davy coughs uncomfortably. He's still dressed in his black funeral garb. I wonder why he's unwilling to tell Harry and I where he really was. "Around noon I had a friend stop in to check in on Hariet. When I left, she looked a little off, and I was worried she might be egg bound. That's when a hen has trouble laying her egg. It's not too fun for the bird, and it is certainly dangerous."

"Did your friend happen to be Dottie?" Harry asks.

There's no denying that a small line of sweat has broken out across Davy's forehead and the pit of his neck.

"Well, now, I don't know about that," Davy stammers.

"It's alright, Davy. Emma and I won't tell anyone about you and her. I was just curious from a timeline perspective." Harry gives him a professional nod. "Let's get back to the vandalism. I assume your friend let you know that someone had egged your chicken coop?"

"They did. They rang me while I was out because they knew where I had gone. I was on my way to go look at it when I found you two outside my house. It couldn't have been better timing either. The sheriff thinks I've fallen off a rock cliff when it comes to my animals going missing, but this here, this is proof that someone has been messing around with my farm!"

Davy stoops down and picks up a large piece of eggshell. "The worst part is they went into my coop and used my own eggs to make this mess. I'll be out here all day trying to scrub the wood so that the egg doesn't bake onto it!"

Davy barks his words out right as a thunderous boom takes over the sky. He looks up and drops the thin shell back onto the ground.

"Maybe we should take this conversation inside," I say. I'm not too keen on standing next to the flimsy barn in the middle of a rough storm. Images of the weakly built frame crashing down on me are not too comforting.

Davy shakes his head. "There's nothing left to talk about. I was right this whole time. Someone is after my farm and my animals. The two of you need to go over to the sheriff's and tell him what's happened. I'd do it myself, but I might get worked up, and I know he's still recovering from his trip to the doctor."

"We would be happy to do that," Harry says. He holds his hand out to shake with Davy's. Davy reciprocates with a begrudging look on his face.

CHAPTER TWENTY-FIVE

A TURN IN THE DAY

As soon as Harry and I get in my car, the heavens rumble deep and long, and lightning flashes across the sky with such violence that both Harry and I jump in our seats. The thunder is followed by rain flowing across the windshield like a translucent curtain. I don't even have a chance to turn my car on before I glimpse Davy through the rain motioning for Harry and I to turn the car off and take cover inside his house.

Harry and I dash through the mud but are still dripping by the time we get to the threshold of Davy's front door. I peel my shoes and jacket off and don't decline the towel Davy tosses my way even though it smells a tad bit like a cat.

"I don't usually take in guests, but I've lived here long enough to know you can't go driving around in a storm like this. It won't last more than a moment, but it's best to wait it out." Davy passes Harry a towel that looks like it has enough holes to be mistaken for some sort of cheese.

Davy takes Harry and I into his kitchen. It's in the back of his house and overlooks the fields. There's not much to it other than a round wooden table and a mismatched wooden chair. Just like the outside of the house, everything is in need of a fresh coat of paint.

I'm not sure what I was expecting from Davy when he invited us inside, but I thought maybe some small talk would occur. True to himself though, Davy doesn't say anything. He stares out the window as the rain wets the landscape before turning to hail.

The pattering of the rain finally gets to me, and I break the tension. "So did you write "Goldfinch of My Heart" in this house?" I ask.

Davy acts like he hasn't heard my question. His dark eyes continue to gaze out the window. Finally, he shifts and faces me.

"I already told you that I don't give interviews," he snaps and turns back to the outside world.

"Why not?" Harry asks. I see that he's cocked his head to the side almost as if he's challenging Davy. I can't help but wonder if he didn't take to the way Davy spoke to me.

"I retired decades ago," Davy says. "How would you like it if all people cared about was something that you did years and years ago? It wouldn't make you feel very good, would it?"

"I guess I never thought of it that way," I say.

Davy has a point. He must be fed up with people obsessing over who he was and not caring anything about who he is today. I know that if I were in the same position, I might feel the same way.

"What if I don't interview you about your music?" I ask. "What if I just interview you as you are today?"

Davy continues to lock his eyes on the forest across the field. I'm not even sure if Mr. Hawking would publish an interview that had nothing to do with "Goldfinch of My Heart," but I can't help but ask Davy for a different kind of interview. Maybe it's my journalistic gut stirring, but I think I could be on to something.

"I suppose that wouldn't be too bad," Davy says. "There's a lot of things I wouldn't mind saying." Davy takes his eyes away from the window to look at me. "I know Melville said you work for a bird magazine, and I wouldn't mind talking about the nature around Goldfinch Gap. That's what I've dedicated my life to since I retired."

I have to keep my composure. The last thing I thought would happen today would be Davy agreeing to give me an interview. I suck in a breath through my teeth and hope that no one notices my nerves that are screaming louder than the thunder outside.

"We could meet in the coffee shop tomorrow morning and talk there? Say around eight?" I suggest.

Davy nods. "I think I would like that."

It might just be the rain running off the windows, but it almost looks as if Davy is getting a bit teary. Maybe going to his brother's funeral stirred something in his heart that made him more willing to talk to me and share his stories.

It's another twenty minutes before the storm has finally left Sourwood. It takes with it gray clouds and heavy air and leaves behind blue sky and the smell of the forest and grass. Harry and I decide to drive back to Charlie's cabin. We need to check in on him after he had such a rough afternoon. We'll stop by the sheriff's tomorrow and tell him about the vandalism on Davy's farm in the morning.

Charlie has migrated from his bedroom to the living room when we get back to the cabin. He's nose deep in a magazine titled *Cheesiest Reading for Cheese Lovers*.

"Feeling better, Charlie?" I ask.

He looks up from his magazine with a big grin. "Everything that happened today is just a small spot in the history of my life. I have had the best news."

"What happened?" Harry takes a seat next to Charlie on the couch. "Did Sheriff Melville call?"

Charlie laughs. "No, something much better! After you two took off, I decided to take my own fieldtrip into town, and I saw that the pharmacy had posted on the window that the shipment of my cheese will be in tomorrow morning!"

"Is this the cheese you drove all the way to Sourwood for?" Harry asks. "The one you were going on about all last night?"

"What other cheese would it be?" Charlie lets out a happy sigh. "And I thought today was the worst day ever. How wrong I was!"

"On that note, I guess I have some good news too," I say. "Davy agreed to give me an interview."

Charlie's mouth drops open. "Does that mean you and Harry solved the murder of Ken Kitson? That was the deal, right? You solve the murder and the sheriff gets you the interview?"

"It was the deal," I reply, "but Davy agreed to the interview without the sheriff's help. Actually, now that Davy has agreed to help me, I suppose that Harry and I don't need to investigate Ken Kitson anymore."

The thought of leaving Ken Kitson's murder unsolved bothers me. I'm not the type of person to come across a problem and leave it, but now that I have my interview with Davy, I really don't need to go poking my nose around Sourwood.

"I can't say the same for myself," Harry says. "When I asked my coworker to help me find Matilda, I had to bring the case to the attention to my work. I'm officially on a job now. I won't be leaving Sourwood until we have as much information about what happened to Ken Kitson as possible."

"Does that mean, come tomorrow, Emma and I will be heading back home, and you'll be stuck in Sourwood?" Charlie asks Harry.

Harry shrugs his shoulders. His eyes peer into mine hopefully. "Personally, I wouldn't mind some extra help."

My heart flutters as if it has wings. I know Harry would help me no matter what, and I know I would do the same for him.

"I'm flattered!" Charlie says. "I'm more than happy to stay and help you, Harry. I know I'm new to this solving murders thing, but I think I'm pretty good at it."

Harry's cheeks turn a bit pink, and I have to cover a giggle with a cough. I know Harry had been asking me to stay and help him and not Charlie. But that doesn't matter. What matters is I've committed to solving Ken Kitson's murder.

Chapter Twenty-Six

Hours at Country Time

When I wake in the morning, any signs of last night's storm have evaporated. The birds are out in the trees singing, and the sky is filled with puffy clouds that remind me of whipped cream. It's warm outside for early spring, so I don't need to take a jacket with me when I leave and head to the coffee shop.

The main street is once again busy with tourists and hikers. The fresh, spring weather has brought people out in large groups. Families push strollers through packs of both young and experienced outdoorsmen. It takes me a few good minutes to find a parking spot within walking distance to Beatrice's coffee shop. I don't mind the extra time it takes me to walk to the shop though. The weather is so beautiful, and the town of Sourwood so charming that it almost feels like I'm dreaming.

When I get to the shop, it's packed as I expected. I have to wait in a long line to order a latte. Beatrice doesn't look overwhelmed with her demanding customers though. She turns sandwiches, muffins, and coffees out quickly. I still can't believe the unassuming woman owns almost all of Sourwood.

I have to wait for a table to free up before I can get a seat. Unfortunately, it isn't the best spot in the restaurant. It's next to the bathroom and is rather drafty. It does remind me of my office at the magazine though, so maybe it'll make me feel more comfortable during my interview with Davy. I take out a notebook and a recorder I brought for the interview. Last night when I returned to the cabin, I had come up with a set of questions I wanted to ask Davy that I thought would be of interest both to him and the magazine's birding readers. I have shivers just thinking about how great this interview will be.

I glance at the time of my phone and see that Davy's late. He had agreed to meet me about fifteen minutes ago. Considering the crowds though, I'm not surprised. I absently doodle a robin in my notebook as I wait for his arrival. So many things have gone wrong in Sourwood, but it's nice that for once something is going right. My stomach squirms in excitement. I had forgotten what it felt like to not be obsessing over trying to score an interview.

My phone buzzes in my purse. It's Mr. Hawking calling to check up on me. Normally, a call from Mr. Hawking would send my inner alarms blaring, but now that I'm on the cusp of an interview that could make my career, confidence surges through my veins.

"Hello," I say.

"Emma, haven't heard from you in a while. How's everything going with Davy Pinesmith? Did you need me to send a photographer down and get some shots? I think Penelope Gray's schedule is finally opening up."

"I'm actually sitting in a coffee shop right now waiting for Davy to show up. Last night, I stopped by his house, and we talked a bit about the specs of the interview. He wanted a piece that focused on where he is now and what he has done for the nature around Sourwood, the little town he lives in and grew up in."

"That's—oh!" There's a jumble of noise on Mr. Hawking's end of the line. "I just spilt half my breakfast on my shirt!" There are a few grumbles and more undiscernible sounds. "I have to go. Send the article when you think it's done. I want it printed ASAP." Mr. Hawking hangs up the phone with a click.

Mr. Hawking wants the article ASAP! He must think it's going to sell a lot of magazines. I can't mess this interview up. I glance down at the time and see that Davy is now twenty minutes late. That's not a huge deal. Twenty minutes of tardiness can be easily explained away. To get my mind off of things, I pull out my birding book and read up on some of the birds I have happened to come across while in Sourwood, but even that does little to distract me. The next glance at the time tells me Davy is now forty-five minutes late. Now I'm concerned. I tell myself I'll wait another thirty minutes. Maybe Davy got the time wrong, and he'll show up here a little after nine.

As the seconds tick by, and my heart beat increases, Davy is still a no show. Around ten, two hours after Davy and I were planning to meet, I give up. I send a text off to Harry to let him know what happened and pack my things away.

While I'm disappointed, a part of me bubbles with annoyance. I should have known that Davy was only playing games when he agreed to an interview with me. He's probably sitting at his farmhouse right now having a good laugh at how easily I fell for his joke. All I've managed to do is make a bigger fool out of myself. I went ahead and gave Mr. Hawking specific details about the interview, and now the interview won't even happen.

I'm on my way back to the cabin when I change routes. I'm not going to let Davy get away with blowing off our interview. It was one thing when he denied me the first interview. He had been overly rude, but the sheriff had been pretending to be him, so I let it slide. But scheduling an interview with me in person and then making me sit in a coffee shop by myself for hours? I'm not afraid of Davy, and I most certainly am not going to allow him to ruin my career. He promised me an interview, and I'm going to go get one.

CHAPTER TWENTY-SEVEN

HIDE AND SEEK

After knocking three times, Davy still doesn't come to answer his front door. An image of him sitting in his kitchen and reading the newspaper as he smirks comes to mind, but I ignore it. I'm not falling for another one of his tricks. I can't believe I ever trusted him and thought he would give me an interview that easily.

The sound of a car driving on the road beyond the house tickles my ears. I turn to see if it might be Davy coming back from some errand, but it's a green, beat-up car driving on the country lane. I start to turn back to the door when my heart skips a beat. It looks like the same car that I had seen at Matilda's, and it could be the same car that Dottie saw parked in Davy's field just the other day. The car slows and turns into Davy's driveway.

There's a large oak tree that has grown close to Davy's house, so I dodge behind it before the driver of the car has a chance to see me. Whoever is behind that green car can't be good news. The car pulls to a stop behind mine, and the tall man exits the vehicle.

I move up against the wide trunk of the tree, hoping that the tall man won't bother to look my way as his long strides take him to Davy's front door. I peer between the lower limbs of the oak tree, expecting to see him knocking on the door just like I was minutes ago, but he bends down and lifts up a corner of the dusty door mat. Underneath it, he grabs a small object, shiny and gold. It's a key.

He uses it to enter Davy's house and closes the door as he disappears inside. I come around from my spot behind the oak and run to get a glimpse through the window above Davy's begonia bed. Unlike the first time I visited his farm, I am careful to not crush any of the colorful flowers under my feet as I look through the window. Past the foggy glass in need of a cleaning, I see that the kitchen is empty. It looks just like it did yesterday with a small exception. The chair that was pulled up next to the table is now sideways on the floor as if someone rose out of it in a quick hurry.

I had been confident that Davy had ditched our interview this morning, but what if something else had happened? What if he had had another incident at the farm? Or worse, what if something had happened to him?

The tall man enters the kitchen and sees the chair on the floor. He studies it for a short second before picking it up. He rifles through some mail that has been left on the table before making his way over to the stove. There's a lone kettle sitting on one of the gas burners. The tall man looks at it for a moment before placing a hand on the side of the kettle.

Something buzzes past my ear—a shallow yelp escapes my lips! A bumblebee is hovering right above my head! The tall man in the kitchen whips his head in my direction, and I dive into the flowerbed. Davy is going to kill me when he sees what his begonias look like now that a full-grown woman has thrown her whole body onto them.

I sneak away from the edge of the window and push myself up so that I'm standing flat against the wall. If the tall man looks out the window, I can't let him see me. But that concern disappears as the front door swings open, and the stranger comes out.

In the far corner of my eye, I spot an opening that looks like it might lead to a crawl space, but it's several yards away from where I stand. I doubt I would make it to the spot quick enough.

The stranger thumps the front door closed with a slam. I don't have much of a choice. I jump onto the ground and crawl towards the opening. I'm not the biggest fan of spiders and other creatures who choose to inhabit dark corners, but I definitely prefer them over getting confronted by a potential murderer.

I shove my feet in first and follow with the rest of my body, twisting myself around until I'm flat against the earth and staring up into the side yard. My one knee rests against a rock uncomfortably, and I feel the sting of scratches up and down my arms. I'm going to be sore tomorrow. That is, if the tall man doesn't discover me here.

As I catch my breath, a pair of men's work boots appear on the grassy patch at the opening of the crawl space. I hold my hand over my mouth. I can't let that man hear my heavy breath. He must know that someone is on the property because of my car parked outside the house, but he doesn't know where I am. I could be out in the fields, nowhere near the old farmhouse.

The boots turn in a circle and walk away towards the front of the house. I strain my ears. If the man goes back inside the house, I'll need to think of where I can head next. I won't be able to move my car if his is still parked behind it.

A car door bangs shut, and the motor ignites. The man must be leaving. I count to sixty seconds before pushing my head out of the opening of the crawl space.

The green car is gone.

I wiggle my way out from under the house and brush the dirt and mud off of my pants and shirt. So much for wearing one of my more professional outfits today. I look more like a scarecrow than a reporter.

I need to get out of here before that man comes back. I very well could have ended up like Ken Kitson had I not been able to hide.

I run towards my car, but pause before reaching it. There's one thing I need to check before I leave Davy's farm.

I hurry up to the front door and lift the corner of the floor mat. It's not as I thought. The mysterious man has left the gold key behind and replaced it exactly where he had found it. Why would he do such a thing?

Chapter Twenty-Eight

CONFRONTATION

"You climbed underneath the house?" Charlie's mouth hangs open as I tell him what I did to avoid being seen by the stranger at Davy's farm. I drove over to Charlie's as soon as I could. I didn't even bother stopping for a shower at my own cabin. I'm covered in mud and have twigs sticking out of my hair.

Harry gently removes a spider web from the sleeve of my sweater. He's calmed down compared to when I first told him about what happened at Davy's house. Initially, Harry had wanted to run over there and search for the stranger himself. "Was Davy there?"

"He never turned up. I really thought he had skipped out on our interview, but now I'm not so sure. What if something happened to him? When I looked into the kitchen, his one chair was on the floor."

Charlie drums his fingers on the cover of a culinary magazine that's on the kitchen counter. I had caught him and Harry about to leave in search of some of the special cheese, but they abandoned their plans when they realized I looked like someone who had just taken a tumble down a hill.

"We should drive over to Sheriff Melville's house. I know he hasn't been the best help so far, but he knows Davy. If there's something uncharacteristic about his behavior this morning, he would know," Harry says.

Charlie looks longingly at the photograph of cheese on the cover of the magazine before sliding the publication away. "Although it hurts me to say it, Davy's possible disappearance is more important than cheese."

Charlie agrees to drive us over to the sheriff's place after its determined that I'm a bit too shaken up to continue driving around. The sheriff and his wife, Polly, are out on their large porch. They appear to be birdwatching as their birdfeeders have attracted quite the array of characters. There is a drab-colored hummingbird, a female, taking nectar from the feeder that hangs just off of the porch, and over at a suet block, a blue jay hangs on the one side while a downy woodpecker eats on the other.

"Isn't it a beautiful morning?" Polly calls to us as we greet her on the porch.

"All those storms sure led to nice weather," the sheriff pipes up. "What brings you three back here?" He takes in my torn jeans and dirty shirt. "Looks like you've been up a good while too."

"We wanted to speak with you about a few things," Harry says as he leans against the porch railing.

"I was talking to Polly about how I'm feeling right as rain," the sheriff says. "Anyways, I wouldn't mind if we all stopped in at my office and went through those reports that Davy had made about the animals on his farm. If you all give me a moment, I can get dressed and meet you downtown."

Polly makes a guttural sound that reminds me of a wolf. The sheriff's cheeks turn a light pink.

"What I mean to ask is if the three of you would wait for me to get changed into my uniform and give me a lift into town? Some people around here," the sheriff glances at Polly, "think I should wait a few more days until I drive again."

Polly rocks back in her chair and takes a sip from her mug, letting out a sigh as she watches a colorful hummingbird hover around the feeder.

"Anyways, what do you three say to that idea?"

"I'd be more than happy to drive everyone into town," Charlie says. "I had some plans to go to the pharmacy. I want to try some of that cheese Sourwood is famous for."

"The cheese the pharmacy gets in every now and then? I doubt any of it will be left," says the sheriff. "You have to get to the pharmacy right at opening to get some of that. It's good, isn't it, Polly?"

"He's right," Polly replies. "We get some once in a while and make ourselves a charcuterie board, but people just about line up outside the door to get it when it comes in."

Charlie's black eyes appear shiny at the news that he may be too late, again, to get some of the cheese he has traveled all the way here for.

It's not long before we're in the sheriff's office. Charlie has disappeared across the street to the pharmacy, determined to find whatever small morsel of cheese has been left behind after the morning crowds. The sheriff has pulled all the files he has on the vandalism related to Davy and spread them out on his desk, creating a collage of black and white paperwork.

"And he never showed?" the sheriff asks me when I finish telling him about my failed interview that morning followed by the incident at Davy's house with the stranger driving the green car.

"I waited two hours," I say.

"I understand your concern, but personally, knowing Davy, I'm not too worried. He has a mind of his own. If he wakes up and decides he doesn't want to do something, he doesn't do it. Why do you think he's never been married? I can't imagine him living happily with someone like Polly bossing him everywhere."

"What about the chair though?" I press the sheriff. "People don't just leave their kitchen chairs on the floor like that."

"And the man who showed up in the car and happened to know where the spare key was?" Harry adds. "You've said it yourself, Davy is a loner, so why would someone be snooping around his house?"

The sheriff shifts in his chair and picks up one of the files on his desk. "Anyways, let's get to business. This here is the first vandalism report that Davy filed."

Harry crosses his arms. His patience with the sheriff is waning.

"Sheriff Melville, do you know who that man was at Davy's house? Emma said he had a green car, a bit older looking, and she also said he was tall."

The sheriff holds up the paper in his hand to eye level so that he can see it better. "The first time Davy came in here, two months ago, he said someone had stolen one of his chickens, Haraldina. It says here that she's a Wyandotte breed with black and white feathers."

Harry takes the paper from the sheriff and sits across from him, placing his elbow on the table and locking his eyes with the sheriff's.

"You asked for our help in solving this case," Harry says in an even, flat voice that I haven't seen him use before, "but Sheriff Melville, you seem to be withholding information from us. I don't think Emma and I can help you unless you tell us everything."

The sheriff leans back in his seat and closes his eyes, taking a moment to think about what he is about to do.

"I suppose you're right. I'll tell you the whole story, this time from the beginning, so that I don't accidently leave anything out."

Chapter Twenty-Nine

An Interview with the Sheriff

"You already know that a few months ago, Davy started coming in here regularly to report funny things going on at his farm. Chickens were being taken, the coop looked like it had been fiddled with, things like that. Those types of incidents aren't uncommon on a farm that borders a forest given the number of foxes and bears in the area along with other predators, so I took the reports down and filed them, as you can see here, but I didn't think anything of it.

"Not too long after Davy started making reports, I was in here on a Saturday morning. The weather was unseasonably warm. It was just like it is today. Anyways, I got a call from a few hikers who were up on Goldfinch Gap. They had come across a body.

"In all my time in Sourwood, I've never had a murder, so I went ahead and made a call to some of the other nearby towns to see if they would give me a hand. They said they would, and we all headed up to the mountain trails. Not long after, one of the nearby departments got an autopsy. Ken Kitson had been hit from behind."

"Did any of the nearby sheriff's departments ever help you with interviews?" Harry asks. His stare is intense, and he looks more like the sheriff than the sheriff does himself.

The sheriff shakes his head. "No. I did all of that. The department that did the autopsy was the same one that identified Ken Kitson, but from there, I tracked down his next of kin and did the interviews."

"What about Davy?" Harry asks. "When did you interview him?"

The sheriff pushes his back against his chair and coughs. "I suppose I would've interviewed Davy on the Monday following the murder."

Harry is silent for a moment. "Where did that interview take place?"

The sheriff itches the top of his nose as he thinks. "I saw Davy in the coffee shop when I chatted with him."

"What'd you ask him?" Harry follows up quickly.

"I asked him how he was doing. Things like that." The sheriff scoots his chair into his desk. He can't stop moving around. "Now here, young man, why are you interrogating me?"

"Sheriff Melville, did you have a proper, sit-down interview with Davy after Ken Kitson was found murdered on his property?"

I hold my breath. The tension in the room swirls in the air like dust motes on a sunny day.

"No, I didn't," the sheriff admits. "I didn't need to. I've known Davy for as long as I've known my wife. I know he didn't murder that city chap who was out hiking. Davy is tough, but he's not the murdering type. He's good to his core."

"That's not the point," Harry replies. "Even if Davy is innocent, he still might know relevant information to the case."

The sheriff makes a dismissive gesture. "Davy doesn't know anything about Ken Kitson and his murder. If he did, he would've told me without my asking. Anyways, he has an alibi. You two were with me when Dottie said she was at his house that night."

"But Dottie said Davy had left the house for a few minutes by himself when he thought someone was on his property," I remind the sheriff.

"Yes, but Dottie said Davy was gone all of five minutes. That's not enough time for him to hike all the way to the bottom of Goldfinch Gap and kill a young man and run back and then check his chicken coop." The sheriff lets out a long breath. "I knew from the beginning you two would be suspicious of Davy, but he has nothing to do with Ken Kitson's murder. All Davy wants in life is to be left alone to work on his farm, so the last thing he would do is go murder someone on it and attract a bunch of attention to himself."

"That's right," Harry says. "Davy doesn't want anyone on his farm, and that's perfect motivation behind a murder. Maybe Ken Kitson was the last straw. He saw the man on his property and had it, so he killed him. Maybe Dottie is covering for him. She does appear to be romantically involved with him."

The sheriff's face turns red in frustration. "I know you're a private detective and all, but I stand by my sheriff's instincts."

"But those instincts didn't serve you very well when Matilda Pinesmith went missing, did they?" Harry presses.

"What does that mean?" the sheriff asks, looking mad.

Harry's eyes have turned cold. "It means—"

"Stop," I stand up and look at Harry and the sheriff. I'm not sure if this is some detective interrogation act Harry is pulling, but I don't like it. "We're not going to get anywhere if we don't let the sheriff tell his story."

Harry softens his features. "You're right, Emma. Sorry, Sheriff Melville. I lost myself there. What I was leading up to is that it's more important than ever that you tell us the whole truth because I don't think you know

Davy as well as you think you do, and now that he's possibly gone missing, things might get even more complicated."

The sheriff takes a second to answer. "Apology accepted. As a sheriff, I understand being passionate about a case."

Harry runs a hand through his hair, tussling it. "We appreciate you agreeing to be honest with us," he says to the sheriff. "Emma and I have also been keeping some things to ourselves."

Harry's amber eyes stare down at his lap. What is he about to reveal to the sheriff? My palms turn sweaty while they stay clasped together on the table.

"I've found Matilda Pinesmith, and she's well and alive, and I think your close friend, Davy, has known about her whereabouts all along."

Harry studies the sheriff's face carefully as he delivers this news, but all there is on his face is shock. I now understand what Harry was doing with his line of questioning. He was trying to fluster the sheriff so that his raw emotions would play across his face when Harry delivered the news about Matilda. It's worked, and the sheriff's face only betrays innocence.

"How?" the sheriff says, his eyes lost.

"She lives in a town on the other side of the mountain. She's been going by her married name for almost as long as she's been missing. There's only one way that you wouldn't have been able to discover Matilda living so close to here for so long, and that would be misinformation from the people who were helping to keep her hidden."

The sheriff looks down at his desk. "You think Davy has been helping to keep Matilda hidden for sixty years? But why would he do that?"

"We don't know," Harry says, "but look at the evidence. You knew how close Davy and Patrick were to their sister, would they really have given up looking for her had they not known she was safe all along?"

"I can't argue with you there," the sheriff says.

"If Davy has been keeping such a big secret from you for this long, who knows what else he is hiding?"

The sheriff takes a moment to process everything. "I know inviting Emma down here to help me with Ken Kitson's murder was the right move," the sheriff says. "The two of you have opened my eyes. Let's solve this murder, but this time, let all the facts come to light."

CHAPTER THIRTY

THE PHONE CALL

"I didn't gain much from the interviews I conducted with the people who were close to Ken Kitson. They all had alibis, and they were all rightfully upset about what happened." The sheriff pulls a large file out from a desk drawer and passes it to Harry. "I'll give this to you so that you can go over it with a fine-tooth comb in case I missed anything, which unfortunately, I appear to do often."

Harry takes the file and nods his thanks to the sheriff.

"From there, nothing much else popped up in the case until the two of you came along."

"Other than the continued vandalism at Davy's farm, which may or may not be linked to the murder," I point out.

"Correct," the sheriff says.

"And if those vandalisms are connected to the murder, they could be looked at a couple different ways," Harry says. "First, if we consider Davy as a suspect, then the lack of reported vandalism on the day of the murder suggests that Davy didn't have time to report the sabotage because he was caught up in the murder."

"Or," I say, "the vandal is the murderer. Dottie said someone had slashed the wire on the chicken coop around the same time that Davy saw someone wandering on his property."

"Either way," the sheriff says, "the pattern is suspicious."

The sheriff is right. The only reason that the vandalism can be linked to the murder in the first place is because of its pattern, which brings to my mind the most recent incident on Davy's farm, the egging of the back of his chicken coop.

"The pattern was broken yesterday too," I tell Harry and the sheriff. "Someone broke into Davy's hen house while he was out, which means his farm was hit two days in a row, something that hasn't happened before."

"Davy didn't contact me yesterday about anything," the sheriff replies.

"That's because we told him we would tell you about it. When Harry and I stopped over there last, he showed us the damage to his chicken coop." I sit up straighter in my seat. "And, while Davy was away from his farm, Dottie had stopped by to check in on him and saw someone wandering around his property. That someone happened to fit the description of the man I saw on Davy's property today."

"So that means the tall man who drives the green car very well could be our vandal and our murderer. We just need to identify him," Harry turns to look at the sheriff.

The sheriff places his hands on his desk. Is he finally willing to tell us the truth now that he knows Davy isn't as honest as he once thought? The sheriff tenses his jaw. "That's a dead end, I'm afraid. Based on your description, the man you're describing is Peter Pinesmith."

"Davy has a son?" I ask.

"No, he has a nephew. Peter Pinesmith is Patrick's son. He comes up here once in a while to check on Davy, and ever since the murder on the property, he's been stopping by more frequently."

"Wouldn't Dottie have known that the man wandering around Davy's property was his nephew? She was the one who was concerned about the man in the first place."

"Davy is private, as you two very well know. He might not have told Dottie about his nephew if he didn't think it was relevant to their relationship."

The sheriff's answer makes sense. After Eleanor had told us that Dottie had seen the tall man in Davy's field, Harry and I had found a pamphlet for Patrick's funeral near some tire tracks. If Peter was Patrick's son, it would make sense for him to have attended the funeral. Knowing that someone had been vandalizing his uncle's farm, Peter must have been making regular stops to check on it. When I had asked Davy if Dottie had been the one to tell him something was wrong at the farm, he had avoided the question, but maybe it wasn't because Dottie had been the one to call, maybe it was because it had been Peter, and he hadn't felt like explaining his relationship to Harry and me.

The phone on the sheriff's desk rings, causing the sheriff to startle in his seat. "That rarely happens," he says before answering the phone and taking the call.

As he listens to whoever is on the other line, his round cheeks sink into his face, and his lively eyes darken. The sheriff bids goodbye to whoever is on the other end of the receiver before hanging up the phone.

"Do you two think your friend Charlie would give us a lift?" The sheriff looks expectantly at Harry and me. "We've got a new lead on the case."

CHAPTER THIRTY-ONE

THE WOMAN ON THE OTHER SIDE OF THE MOUNTAIN

"That punk-teenager who works at the pharmacy told me that they were all sold out, and he showed me the empty refrigerator section," Charlie says as he takes a sharp turn on the mountain road.

I have no idea where we are going. The sheriff had enough time to give Charlie an address to plug in the GPS before Charlie launched into the long-version of the story behind why he still is not in possession of Sourwood's specialty cheese.

"Harry, I see you eyeing the GPS. I already told you I downloaded the directions offline when we left, so it's okay if the reception skips out," Charlie's eyes are reflected in the rearview mirror as they glare at Harry.

Harry turns his head to stare out the window at the passing trees and the exposed limestone jutting out of the carved mountains. I thought Harry had been nervous when I was driving in the mountains because I was riding the brakes, but now I wonder if he's just a nervous passenger in general.

The trees thin a bit, and we're finally over the mountains. A small town comes into view with a vet clinic and gas station. It's the same one that Harry and I drove through to get to Matilda's house. I exchange a look with Harry and see that he is thinking the same thing I am. What are the chances that the sheriff's new lead happens to somehow be connected to Matilda?

As quickly as we enter the town, we exit, continuing on to another stretch of road. Beads of sweat populate my brow as we roll by houses with colorful gardens and unique mailboxes. We're on the same street that Matilda lives on.

Harry notices too. He gives my hand a comforting squeeze as Charlie pulls right into Matilda's driveway and parks his car in front of the garden gnomes. Their position has changed from yesterday. Instead of circled up, they are spread out in pairs and facing their partners as if they are at a formal dance.

"Sheriff, what exactly happened on that phone call you had?" I ask. Does the sheriff know this is Matilda's house? Had Matilda called him herself?

The sheriff turns his head back from where he sits in the front seat to see me better. "It was an anonymous tip about the Ken Kitson murder. Whoever was on the line said I best check out the people who live at this address."

Harry looks at me, the flecks of yellow in his eyes shining in the sun, and I know we're thinking the same thing. The sheriff is going to be in for a shock when he goes up to the front door and is greeted by Matilda Pinesmith. Although, if she goes by her married name and has changed enough throughout the years, the sheriff might not even know that he's talking to Davy's sister.

We gather behind the sheriff as he firmly knocks on the door. It's odd thinking that Harry and I were doing the exact same thing just yesterday.

The gauzy curtains rustle, and an orange cat pops up onto the windowsill. It stares at the four of us with disinterest, turning around to lick its paw and start a bath.

The door creaks open, and a woman with a long nose and owl-like eyes peeks at the group of us. Her fluffy, gray hair is tucked into the neck of a cardigan, and a pair of readers are sitting on the tip of her nose.

"Yes?" she looks at us, no doubt a slew of ideas running through her head as to why such a mismatched group is at her door.

The sheriff extends his hand. "Ma'am, I'm Sheriff Melville from the other side of the mountain. I would like to speak with you about something that occurred in the town of Sourwood not too long ago. May I come in?"

The woman slowly takes the sheriff's hand and gives it a weak shake. "Come in." She opens the door wider so that the interior of her house can be seen.

It's small and charming. There's a worn, green couch with orange pillows pushed against the far wall which is covered in wallpaper. The brown coffee table has a large doily on it, and a setting for afternoon tea sits on a silver tray. There are two tea saucers. Clearly, Matilda had been expecting company, just not us.

Matilda picks up her large, orange cat and sits down with it in a stiff chair in the corner. It's upholstered in a bright blue pattern that matches the little flower accents on the living room rug.

"Feel free to sit," she gives her orange cat a scratch behind one of its ears.

The sheriff, Harry, and Charlie all situate themselves on the couch while I make myself comfortable in a small, rigid chair near the front door.

"How can I help? I presume you're here on serious business considering who you are," she looks pointedly at the sheriff's badge.

"Unfortunately, we are. I'm not sure if you follow the going-ons in Sourwood?"

Matilda's eyes widen for a millisecond before she readjusts her expression. "I'm not sure I pay too much attention to the news from the other side of the mountain."

"That's to be expected," the sheriff says. "I won't waste too much of your time catching you up on the story, but essentially, a man was killed while hiking in Sourwood, ever heard about it?"

Matilda's lips purse, but she shakes her head. "No. I don't enjoy outdoor activities, so I don't know much about the mountains other than that they are there."

"You still might be able to help me. Earlier today, I received a call saying that you have information about the case," the sheriff continues. "Anyways, maybe you didn't know a man was killed, but maybe someone you know went missing? Or something peculiar happened to you a few months ago? You never know what helps."

Matilda's hand has frozen on the top of her cat mid-pet. Her eyes are wide, and there's no hiding it this time. "Someone called you and said *I* had information about a murder?"

The sheriff makes a passive gesture with his hands. "Not you specifically, but someone who lives at this address."

"The only other person who lives here is my husband, but if he knew something about a murder, he would've said something."

From the corner of my eye, I see that Harry is on the edge of his seat. He's probably trying to find the perfect time to ask Matilda about her identity.

Matilda's cat nudges her immobile hand with its nose to get more pets. "The caller must've been mistaken, especially if they didn't even leave a name."

Harry leans forward, barely any seat cushion left to prevent him from hitting the floor. "Actually, we're happy you brought that up. My name is Harry Starling, and I work for a private detective business. I'm helping

Sheriff Melville with the case. For the record, could we have your name since we've been interviewing you?"

"Matilda Pierton," Matilda says. "Would you like me to spell it? Some people have a hard time with the spelling of the last name."

"That won't be necessary," the sheriff staggers to his feet. "It seems whoever called my office was mistaken. We apologize for taking up your time."

Harry stands up and steps in front of the sheriff. "And your maiden name?"

The sheriff gives Harry an odd look.

"For the records," Harry says quickly.

Matilda freezes as her cat jumps from her lap. "Pardon?" she asks.

"Could we get your maiden name for the records?" Harry smiles at her, showing off a charming dimple.

Matilda looks down at her hands. "Pinesmith," she whispers.

The sheriff stumbles backward onto the couch, but not much mind is given to him because at that moment, the front door opens.

CHAPTER THIRTY-TWO
A FAMILY VISIT

P eter Pinesmith stands in the doorway. I've only seen him from afar. Close up, I can see the strong resemblance between him and Davy from the photographs of Davy when he was younger. Like Davy once had, Peter has sandy blond hair and a wide mouth.

He looks around the room at the group of us squished into the tiny living room along with the cat who is pawing at Charlie.

"Everything okay, Aunt Matilda?" he asks.

Matilda reaches out and scoops up the cat so that it leaves Charlie alone and is once again nestled in her lap. She's recovered from her earlier panic. "Sheriff Melville and his friends were visiting because they had an anonymous tip that someone who lived at this address was associated with a murder."

Peter raises his eyebrows. "Is this about the murder of Ken Kitson?"

Matilda grabs tight onto her cat as it tries to leap to the floor.

"It is," Harry extends his hand to Peter and introduces himself. "Have you and your aunt heard about it?"

Peter scoffs and tilts his head in a way that pushes his sandy hair out of his eyes. "Without a doubt we know about it."

Harry looks at Matilda, her story falling apart like sand through a sieve.

"Oh, was the murder of the hiker the Ken Kitson murder? Then I have to revise my answer. Yes, I have heard about that." Matilda sends a firm hand down the spine of her cat who has extended its claws, trying to get out of her grip.

Peter gives his aunt an odd look.

"You're Matilda Pinesmith," the sheriff says in disbelief as he stares at Matilda.

The sheriff has recovered from the news of Matilda's identity. He is now sitting up straight on the couch. I'm thankful that Harry had told him about Matilda's existence before the anonymous call at his office. I can't imagine how well the sheriff would've taken the news that Matilda was sitting right in front of him, petting a cat, had he still thought she was a missing person.

Matilda doesn't answer the sheriff's question because Peter speaks. "Yes, and I'm her nephew, Peter Pinesmith. We've been waiting some time for the sheriff's office to stop by here."

"You've been waiting for me to come by here?" the sheriff asks. "How was I to know I needed to come around here?"

"Isn't that your job?" Peter asks before making another scoffing sound from the back of his throat.

I bite down on my lip. Technically, Peter isn't wrong. It *was* the sheriff's job to find Matilda Pinesmith, but it's a tad bit awkward to phrase it that way.

"No one has bothered to contact me since the murder of Ken Kitson. I've had to get all of my information from my Uncle Davy," Peter continues. "Even while my father was alive, I had power of attorney, and this is the first time that the sheriff's office has shown up here."

I know I'm not the only person in the room having trouble following what Peter is saying. Why would the sheriff had needed to contact him after

Ken Kitson's murder? Had Peter known Ken Kitson? But what does that have to do with the power of attorney?

Charlie is the first one to break the trance of confusion. "I get it!" He claps his hands together loudly. "Everyone knew that the Pinesmiths owned the land that Ken Kitson was found on, but everyone incorrectly *assumed* Davy owned the parcel where Kitson's was killed. Patrick was the one who really owned it, and now that he's dead, his son owns it."

Peter isn't impressed by Charlie's outburst. "Who are you?"

"Charlie Kim," he answers with a smile. "This is my first murder case."

Peter turns back to the sheriff. "Did the sheriff's office not realize that my father, Patrick, owned the portion of land where Ken Kitson was found? I thought who the land belonged to would've been one of the first things the office looked into."

The sheriff shrugs his shoulders apologetically. "Sourwood isn't adequately staffed for crimes like this. There's a reason I need outside help." He motions to Harry and me.

"Now we know why Davy is so rude whenever anyone tries to talk with him about what happened to Ken Kitson on his land. It was never his land," Charlie says unhelpfully.

"I have to get going," Peter says. "I was just dropping by to grab something from the guestroom. I'm going to assume that the sheriff's office will contact me at a later time to discuss the case? I don't imagine anyone here has prepared anything to discuss with me at the present time?"

"Nope," the sheriff admits.

Peter repeats the tilting motion he used earlier to get his hair out of his eyes. "I'll be staying here for another week, so you know where to find me." Peter exits the room to go down a hall.

Harry is the first to talk. "I think it's fair to say that while it's been revealing to learn who the true owner is of the property, there is another conversation that needs to be had here."

Matilda finally lets go of her orange cat, letting it dash under the couch.

"I really thought no one would ever find me. It seems that I've been caught through a fluke, someone gave you a wrong address, and here I am," Matilda twists her hands together.

"I suppose you want to know why I disappeared," she says quietly.

"That would be helpful," Harry replies softly.

"Let's see. It was about sixty years ago. I was young, very young, and tired, very tired." Matilda sighs as her eyes take on a faraway look. "Davy and Patrick knew that I was in trouble and that I needed to leave Sourwood. We had thrown different ideas around like me going on tour with Davy, but logistics always got in our way. Eventually, we decided to stage a kidnapping that would let me get away, but not too far. You see, I would've missed my brothers too much if I had traveled."

Matilda takes a stilted breath. "So, Davy and Patrick helped me escape one night and then reported me missing to the sheriff's department." Matilda glances at the sheriff. "I presume you remember the case?"

"I do," the sheriff says. "I found a piece of cloth in the woods from that night, and for years it bothered me because it was neatly cut from a larger piece of fabric, and not something that should've been present at a kidnapping scene."

"Patrick planted that. I told him it wasn't needed, but he wouldn't listen."

"Does your nephew, Peter, know that you're a missing person?" Harry asks.

Matilda shakes her head. "I would prefer if you didn't tell him either. It all happened so long ago. I don't see the point in bringing it up."

"Why did you do it?" Harry leans into the pillows of the couch, acting as if this conversation is just about the mail or the weather.

Matilda is quiet for a moment. "It was a silly reason. My boyfriend at the time had betrayed me with a close friend. I was so embarrassed I asked Davy and Patrick to get me as far from Sourwood as they could manage. It turns out I didn't get very far." Matilda offers us a closed-mouth smile. "Sorry if you were hoping for a more interesting story."

Peter pokes his head into the room from the hallway. He's changed his clothes and has a red backpack slung over one shoulder. "Is everything alright, Aunt Matilda?"

"Just peachy," Matilda replies.

"We should get going," Harry stands. "We appreciate your time, Mrs. Pierton."

There are a thousand more questions running through my mind, but I have no time to ask them. Harry is already out the door, and Charlie is on his heels. I glance back and give Matilda a tiny wave, but she ignores me in favor of scratching her cat's ears.

My gut aches. There's no way Matilda told us the truth. I don't believe for one moment that Davy would've gone to the lengths he did to hide Matilda to only save her a bit of embarrassment.

As Charlie's car whips by the blossoming trees in their spring pinks and yellows, there's no discussion. We're all lost in a sea of thoughts. Something doesn't seem right. There's another reason that Davy helped his sister disappear, and I'm going to figure out what that reason is.

Chapter Thirty-Three

GAME NIGHT

Charlie plops a large piece of lasagna onto my plate. The kitchen at his rental is rich with the aroma of basil and tomatoes. It's already dusk, and only a little light breaks its way through the forest canopy that shelters the cabin.

After Charlie dropped the sheriff off at his house, we went back to Charlie's to discuss what we had discovered during our visit with Matilda. Harry and I had sat at the kitchen counter, brainstorming ideas, while Charlie had thrown together a lasagna with the ingredients he had in the refrigerator.

"It's a bummer that your interview fell through with Davy," Charlie says as he puts a large slice of lasagna on a plate for Harry. "But based on what you two told me, the sheriff didn't seem to think much of it, did he?"

"I still think we should check on him," Harry runs his knife through the center of his slice of lasagna, sending thick sauce oozing onto his plate. "The sheriff has a good heart, but there's been too many mishaps in this case. I would hate for something to happen to Davy right under our noses."

"You can count me out," Charlie cuts into his own lasagna slice. "The last time Emma went over there, she ended up hanging out in a crawl space. That doesn't sound like a fun vacation excursion for me."

"In my defense, I didn't know who Peter Pinesmith was at the time when I was hiding from him. If he were to pop up again on Davy's property, I think I would go for a greeting and a hello instead of bolting under the house." I put a piece of the lasagna in my mouth. It's soft and flavorful, the cheese and tomato sauce melting together on my tongue.

"Even more reason not to go over to Davy's again. Peter wasn't what I would call pleasant," Charlie says.

"I can't argue with that," Harry bites into the lasagna for the first time. "Charlie, this is amazing! I forgot how good your cooking was."

Charlie makes a dismissive gesture. "It's nothing, really."

Harry's right. Charlie has a touch when it comes to cooking, but he won't take any compliments. His career as a food critic means most of what he eats has been created by some of the best chefs in the world, so he never believes his homemade grub is anything special.

"I'm planning to head into town early tomorrow and check in at the pharmacy to see if there's any cheese," Charlie says. "I can't keep missing out on the opportunity to get some. The cheese is going to have to be my main priority."

"It's odd that it is sold in the pharmacy, isn't it?" Harry takes a sip of his water.

"I thought so too, but there aren't really any grocery stores in Sourwood, so I think the pharmacy serves as an all-stop shop rather than a traditional pharmacy," I say.

"You two will want to take Emma's car when you go check on Davy in the morning. I'll be on my cheese errand." Charlie wipes his mouth with a napkin.

"That won't be an issue," Harry says once he's finished chewing on a large piece of lasagna. "I think we should check on Davy tonight. Better now than later."

The bit of lasagna I had been eating suddenly feels limp and rubbery in my mouth. "Tonight?"

For some reason the idea of skulking around Davy's farm at night isn't the most appetizing. Someone has been vandalizing the property on a regular basis, and that person very well could be a murderer.

"When you went and checked on Davy in the morning, there were countless places he could have been, but during nightfall nothing is open in Sourwood, so if he's not at home, we'll know something is wrong," Harry says.

As much as I don't want to go traipsing around Davy's at night, Harry does have a good point.

"What time will we leave then?" I scrape the last bits of food off my plate.

Harry checks his watch. "I would say in about an hour. That would make it a little too early for Davy to be in bed, but too late for him to be out and about."

Charlie rinses off his dish in the sink. "Count me out. I think I'm done with excitement for the day. You two forget, this is the first time I've helped you solve a murder." Charlie places the dish on a drying rack. "Also, I need to be up bright and early for my cheese mission."

"Cheese mission?" Harry asks as he dunks his own dirty plate into the soapy water.

"That's what I'm calling it," Charlie replies. "My cheese mission. It's the working title for the article I am going to write once I get my hands on the cheese. Speaking of articles," Charlie pauses and looks at me, "how is your article coming along, Emma?"

Heat creeps into my cheeks. "It's coming along as good as an article comes along when the main person being interviewed won't talk to me."

My cellphone feels warm in my pocket. I haven't looked at it almost the whole day, and I have no doubt that there are messages and emails on there waiting for me from Mr. Hawking. Today is Monday, so Mr. Hawking was no doubt flitting around the office, waiting for my article to come in as the hours ticked by. He might even still be sitting at his desk right now, hoping I send him a late submission. If I don't get that interview with Davy soon, I might not have a job to come back to. And last I checked, bird journalists weren't in high demand. I try to forget about my phone for now.

After dinner, Charlie convinces us all to play one of the board games he found in the cabinet by the television to pass the time. The game involves trying to land your character on different colored squares around a castle by doing some type of math. I'm not very good at it, and the game seems to prolong the minutes rather than shorten them. Harry insists that we keep playing despite Charlie's protests that the game is "wonky," but I think Harry only wants to keep playing because he's winning. Finally, Harry's character masters some equation of sorts and seizes the castle from the goblins.

"That was fun!" Harry says as he places the small game pieces back into the box.

"That's because you took out all those trolls so early. In fact, I think that's the only reason you won." Charlie nudges me in the ribs.

Harry rolls his eyes playfully. "You're just mad because you answered that one question wrong, so your character got turned around at the Swampy Swirl."

Charlie closes the top of the box and mimics Harry as he slides the game onto the shelf. I don't think we'll be playing that game again soon. At least I hope we won't.

"It's time for us to get a move on to Davy's. The two of you ready?" Harry slings on the light jacket that he had folded on the back of his chair. The light brown in the fabric brings out the color of his eyes. If Charlie wasn't standing in the room with us right now, I would probably give Harry a kiss.

"I think I'll come back here after I drop you two off," Charlie says. "You need someone to run backup. I'll wait around here, and if the two of you haven't called me by midnight, I'll go looking."

"We'll definitely be back here before midnight," I say. "I have no intentions of hanging out on Davy's farm any longer than we have to."

"It's not about you staying there because you want to. There's a murderer on the loose, and you two are about to frolic around the crime scene," Charlie says.

Charlie's not wrong. This little outing might end up being very dangerous.

"I'll give you that one, Charlie." Harry slips into his shoes by the door.

As I'm doing the same, an idea strikes me. Davy is so evasive of my attempts to interview him, what if visiting him tonight is my one chance to finally get him talking? If the sheriff is right and Davy blew off our interview because he had something better to do today, there might be a strong chance that he'll agree to the interview tonight now that he has no errands to run.

"Charlie, do you mind if we stop by my cabin before we go to Davy's farm?" I ask. "I want to pick up some notes I left there. You never know what might happen, and if Davy is willing, tonight could be the night I finally get my interview."

"That shouldn't be a problem," Charlie opens the door for us. "In fact, I can drop you at your cabin, and you and Harry can drive over to Davy's without me. That way, you don't need to call me to pick you up."

Charlie locks up the cabin as Harry and I wait by the car. The outside lamp has been left burning bright on the porch, so a collection of moths and other bugs of the night are swarming around it. The only sounds that can be heard are the little taps of the bugs bouncing off the glass protecting the lightbulb.

Charlie honks his car in goodbye as he peels out onto the country road and away from my cabin. Above our heads, the sky is a map of twinkling stars with only the occasional cloud to block the view. It's stunning. Harry notices it too. He wraps me up in a hug as we stand there, awestruck.

"I know this wasn't the weekend you were looking forward to," he says, his breath tickling the thin skin of my ear.

"I don't think this was the weekend anyone was looking forward to, but I'm happy you're here." I lay my head against his chest.

He gives me a tight squeeze and tugs me towards the cabin. "We don't have much time. Let's get your keys and notes and head over to the farm."

We enter the cabin, and close the door before flicking on the light. I don't want any of the bugs following us inside. I grab my notebook where it is resting on the kitchen table. A pen that was on top of it rolls onto the floor and makes a clinking sound when it hits the wood. I bend down and grab it, but my mouth curves into a frown.

"What's wrong?" Harry asks.

"This isn't my pen," I hold it up so that Harry can see better. It's green, and on the side is printed the words *Sourwood Bakery: Fresh and Hot.*

"Maybe you accidently picked it up when you went to the bakery to grab something to eat? Or maybe you grabbed it when you were at the coffee shop, and someone else had left it there?"

I twirl the pen between my fingers, positive that I haven't seen it before, but also aware that I'm being ridiculous. People pick up pens accidently all the time. The fact that Sourwood has an unsolved murder is just freaking me out.

"You're probably right," I put the pen down. "Let's get going."

Harry's cellphone rings, and he pulls it out of his jacket pocket. "It's Charlie."

"Hello?" Harry answers. Immediately his eyebrows pull together. "Slow down, Charlie. I can't understand what you're saying. Emma and I are still at her cabin. We'll be there right away."

Harry hangs up the phone. "We need to go back to Charlie's. I'm not sure what happened, but he's in a panic."

I grab my keys from the counter and run out to my car. Between the written warnings I've been getting, Harry's slashed tires, and the vandalism at Davy's farm, a number of bad things could have happened to Charlie. Harry and I need to get to his rental as fast as possible. He could be hurt or in trouble.

I get to my car door, and try to jam the key into the lock to get inside, but it doesn't fit. I'm so nervous that my hands are trembling.

"What's wrong?" Harry runs up next to me.

"Just nerves," I go to unlock my car again, but once again, the key doesn't go in the lock.

"Let me try," Harry says, gently prying the keys from my hand.

He tries to enter the key in the lock as I did earlier, but again, it doesn't fit. He pulls his phone out and accesses the flashlight app to better examine the key.

"Emma, this isn't your key," he murmurs under his breath.

What Harry says doesn't register. "Of course it's my key. Whose key would it be if it wasn't mine? I'm the only one staying in the cabin, and that's my house key linked up to my keychain." I point out the silver key next to my car key as well as the cardinal keychain.

"Look at the car key insignia. It doesn't match your car make."

Harry's right. The key has some sort of triangle insignia printed on it that doesn't match my car. My car key was taken off of my keychain and replaced with a random key!

"Someone was definitely in the cabin," I say. "I left my keys in there today when we were out because I knew I wouldn't need them," my whispers are rushed.

Harry looks off into the woods before protectively placing his hand on the small of my back. "Pack a bag for the night, and I'll make a call to Charlie. I don't think you should be staying in this cabin alone. Someone doesn't want us in Sourwood, and they'll do anything to make us leave."

CHAPTER THIRTY-FOUR

A BROKEN LIGHT

Harry, Charlie, and I are gathered around the coffee table in the living room. It's odd thinking that the last time we were here we had been playing a game that involved trolls and goblins. Now, the mood is morose and heavy. Charlie is wrapped up in a blue and white blanket with a cup of tea balanced on his knee.

"I don't know how I'll be able to sleep," he says.

"Explain what happened again, but this time slower," Harry says to Charlie. He has his knees tucked under him and dark circles are ringing his eyes.

Charlie had told us a rushed, frantic story when he picked us up from my cabin, but both Harry and I had a hard time understanding it since our minds were lost on the break-in.

"Shortly after you left, probably ten minutes, there was a big bang outside. I was in the kitchen, soaking the lasagna pan when I heard it." Charlie says in rushed breath. "At first, I thought someone had shot at the cabin, that's how loud it was. I jumped for cover under the kitchen table."

"That's awful," I give Charlie's shoulder a pat.

"Eventually, I crawled out and found my phone and called Harry. I had retreated back under the table when Harry called back and told me that I was going to have to go and pick you two up at your cabin." Charlie's voice trembles a bit at the memory.

"I made my way out on the porch when I realized that it was pitch dark. I couldn't even see the stars through the trees. It was like being in a cave. I even tripped over a large rock on the porch. That's when I realized," Charlie holds his hands out to emphasize the realization that hit him. "I hadn't heard a shot from a gun. No, someone had thrown a rock at the porch light, and as the rock cascaded off the wall and broke the glass, it had created a loud crack."

"That makes four of us then," Harry rubs his temples in frustration. "My tires were slashed, the porch light was hit while Charlie was the only one in the cabin, Emma has gotten threatening notes, and Davy Pinesmith has someone sabotaging his farm. Someone is angry."

"Do you think that angry someone is the same person who attacked Ken Kitson?" I ask.

"It has to be, doesn't it?" Charlie says. "Why else would someone want the three of us to leave town so badly?"

"It's a possibility, but we can't know for sure yet." Harry stretches his hands across a pillow he is holding in his lap and eyes his watch. "I think it's too late to check up on Davy. We'll have to do it sometime tomorrow."

"Emma, let me show you to the empty guestroom," Charlie tosses his blanket on the couch.

Harry stays downstairs while I follow Charlie up the staircase. The cabin is so well constructed that not even one of the dark wood steps squeaks on our way up. The hallway on the top floor is short but wide. Dark paintings of sea storms decorate the light gray walls between black doors that lead to the bedrooms. There must be a trick to the lighting. Everything appears sleek and new and bright.

Charlie goes to the end of the hall and opens the last door, unveiling a room with plush carpet and a large sleigh bed.

"I hope this will do," he says.

"It looks like it jumped out of a magazine." I set my bag on the carpet.

Charlie shrugs. "It's not too shabby for a cabin. I'll leave you to it." He closes the door behind him.

I change into a pair of pajamas and get into bed, plugging my phone into a nearby charger before shutting off the lights. The screen lights up when it registers the charging cord, and I have five missed calls and several text messages. A few are from my parents, one from Charlie, but the rest are all Mr. Hawking.

Instead of opening the texts and listening to the voicemails, I set my phone on the nightstand and turn it so that the screen is facing down. Someone has spent the last few days sending me mean notes, today they were in my cabin, taking my key, and Davy didn't show up for our interview. I can't handle an ounce more of bad news.

I get on my stomach and push my hands under the over-fluffed pillow. Unlike at my cabin, the room is dead silent. Despite being in the middle of the woods, I can't hear any owls hooting or foxes crying. I wonder what the point is of soundproofing a house in the middle of the forest.

After listening to the silence for almost an hour without a wink of sleep, I head downstairs for a glass of water. When I do reach the kitchen, there is movement outside the window. I scurry over to get a better look and arrive just in time to see a rambunctious racoon flop to the ground before running into the nearby trees.

"I'm surprised you're up," Harry says from the living room, making me jump.

I take a deep breath to steady myself. "I couldn't sleep." I grab a clean glass and fill it with water from the tap.

"I never even tried to. I knew my mind would be loud with ideas after today." Harry fiddles with something in his hand. As I get closer, I see that it's the impersonation key that had been switched out with my real key.

"Any thoughts?" I sink onto the couch next to him, laying my head on his shoulder.

"Let me see," he glances over at me. "I think you look beautiful even when you can't sleep."

I smile and look up into Harry's eyes. "You know that's not what I meant."

Harry sighs. "I know."

"So, what is actually keeping you up?"

Harry twists the key around in his hand. "What type of lock does your cabin have on it?"

"The same type as Charlie's," I reply. "You press in a code and gain access to the rental. I think those are pretty standard these days."

Harry leans his head back on the couch. "No sign of forced entry, no possibility of a spare key being discovered in a hiding spot, so someone knows that code to your cabin."

I frown. "I hadn't thought about that. How would someone get the code?"

"Maybe they stayed at the rental before you did, and the property owner never bothered to update the key code?"

I sit up straight. "That could mean that if we find out who stayed in the cabin around the same time that Ken Kitson was murdered, we could, theoretically, have another lead to follow." I bite down on my lip. "But how would we figure out who rented the cabin before I did?"

"We could contact the owner and ask," Harry says. "Do you have access to the rental app?"

"Unfortunately, no. The sheriff made my reservation for me. He would have all that information, and I doubt he's awake right now."

"It gives us something to do in the morning," Harry says and covers a big yawn with his hand.

I snuggle up beside him and wrap my arms around his waist. "Do you think we'll ever find out what happened to Ken Kitson?"

For a moment I think Harry has fallen asleep. With his head tilted back on the sofa and his eyes closed, he looks like he's drifted away. He hasn't though. He turns and gives the top of my head a small kiss.

"I think that only time will tell, but we have one big advantage over the person doing all these things," Harry says.

I raise my eyebrows.

"We have no secrets to hide."

CHAPTER THIRTY-FIVE

FAMILY CONNECTIONS

The line at Beatrice's coffee shop stretches all the way into the street. I've never seen anything like it before, not even when I've visited my sister in the city. Harry and I wait patiently behind a large man with a mountainous beard and furry ears. Charlie isn't with us because he's gone to scout out the pharmacy in case some cheese was delivered last night. He had agreed to drive Harry and I into town this morning, but only after sternly reminding us that the cheese mission was his number one priority.

The line moves an inch closer to the door. This time, Harry and I are waiting by the window to the shop. I glimpse a large group of hikers at the counter. They talk for a long time, ordering a large amount of food before they set out on their trek. Beatrice nods her head as she listens to the order. Her eyes have dark circles under them, and her auburn hair is frizzy in her bun. She must be overworked.

"I think it will be a while before we get inside," I say to Harry. "Maybe we should hop over to the bakery and see if they have pastries or something."

"I'm okay with that."

Harry and I leave our place in line behind and cross the street. Like yesterday, the weather is beautiful. The flower pots that sit outside the shop doors are in full bloom, and little, purple crocuses dot the grassy areas where small trees have been planted along the sidewalk. I find myself imagining living in Sourwood as a local, and a pleasant feeling blooms in my chest.

Harry opens the door to the bakery for me, and I go inside. The smell of warm bread greets us. Unlike the coffee shop, the bakery is large and airy. Tall windows shine bright light into the space, and tables are sporadically set up around the area. Harry goes up to the glass case by the register and looks at the variety of cookies, pastries, and sliced loaves available for purchase.

A woman comes from out of the back room and greets us. She looks to be in her forties. "Morning!" Her voice is jolly. "Anything interest you? We have a special today on banana bread. Buy a loaf and get a free lemon berry cookie."

"Tempting, but we're more in the mood for breakfast," Harry says. He flashes a wide smile at the woman, and she smiles right back at Harry.

"I've got some fresh biscuits in the back. They go well with a drizzle of honey and butter. Would that work?"

My stomach grumbles at just the thought of warm biscuits with a generous spread of butter on them. Harry must be thinking the same because he orders two for us at the counter. We grab a seat by one of the windows and watch the line at Beatrice's coffee shop grow longer by the second.

"It's nice in here. I'm happy we stopped in," I say, looking at the colorful art decorating the wall.

"There's no way we would've been able to grab a seat at Country Time Coffee," Harry says.

The woman from behind the counter comes over to our table and places two plates in front of us. The biscuits she has brought out are the size of my fists. "I brought you some tea on the house as well." She places an artful teapot on the table with a collection of teacups. The set is decorated delicately with painted pink rose petals and yellow birds that look like goldfinches.

"Thanks so much," I say. "It all looks delicious."

"No problem," the woman gushes, tucking a piece of her hair behind her ear, revealing a large pearl earing. "Are you two in town for the hiking trails?"

"In a way, yes," Harry says while pouring a steaming cup of tea.

"I love all the visitors that drop in through our little town. My family has been here forever, and the place has changed so much since I was a kid. I think it's just wonderful." The woman tucks another loose strand of hair behind her ear. "I'll be behind the counter if you need anything."

"She was friendly," Harry says right before biting into his biscuit. He lets out a groan as he chews. "These are amazing."

I can't agree more. The biscuit is buttery, salty, and soft. All its savory flavors mix with the sweet tang of honey.

"We should tell Charlie to come here and try these," I say and take another large bite. "Do you think he'll be done at the pharmacy soon?"

Harry doesn't hear me though. His eyes are locked on the woman behind the counter. She rearranges a few pastries in the case so that she can add some bread loaves to the display.

"You okay?" I ask him. "Did you want to get something else to eat?"

Harry puts his biscuit down on his plate. "I just had an idea. Remember that old prom picture I showed you?"

"The one with Matilda?"

"Remember how there were two other people in the photo? Finneas Ransom and Ella Worle?"

"What about them?" I put my own biscuit on my plate. Harry's line of questioning awakens my curiosity. Somehow the biscuit that had seemed so important only a moment ago is now a thought left behind.

"Doesn't that lady behind the counter remind you of someone?" Harry whispers.

I look back at the woman as she reaches her hand into the display and places a sign in front of a small batch of cookies and muffins that says *half-off day-old goods*. As she stands back up, a piece of her hair falls over her shoulder, and I see what Harry is talking about. The woman looks uncannily like an older version of Ella Worle, the best friend of Matilda who had cheated with Finneas Ransom.

"That can't be Ella," I whisper to Harry. "Ella would be in her late seventies by now."

"She said her family has lived in Sourwood for years," Harry's voice is just a hush. "Maybe it's Ella's daughter or a niece?"

Harry is on to something. When we had confronted Matilda about her disappearance, the reason Matilda gave us for doing what she did was unbelievable. It's hard to imagine even the most dramatic of teenagers staging their own kidnapping as a reaction to a tough breakup. Talking to someone related to Ella might give us enough context to figure out the real reason that Matilda went missing all those years ago.

"Anything else I can get you?" the woman behind the counter says, pasting on another big smile. Harry and I must've been staring.

"Actually, yes," Harry says. "Is there a chance that you're related to Ella Worle?"

I bite my lip. Harry has really taken a chance. We don't even know the first name of this woman, and we're asking her about her family.

The woman laughs while she comes out from behind the counter and puts a tea towel into the pocket of her apron. "I haven't heard my mother called Ella in quite some time. How do you two know her? She doesn't usually mix with tourists."

"We don't know her exactly. We more so had questions about her," Harry says.

The woman's face takes on an inquisitive look. "I'll try my best. I didn't know my mother was interesting enough to elicit the attention of strangers. The two of you have me curious." She sits down at our table and scootches her chair closer to me. "My name is Janet, by the way."

Harry and I introduce ourselves.

Leaning forward in his seat, Harry softens the hard angles of his face as he addresses Janet, "Did your mother ever talk to you about someone named Finneas Ransom or maybe Matilda Pinesmith? Specifically, did she ever mention being in a relationship of sorts with Mr. Ransom?"

Janet's face turns bright red. For a moment, I think she's about to tell us to leave her establishment, but I'm mistaken. She bursts into hysteric giggles. "You have to excuse me," she says, wiping an escaped tear from her eye. "The thought of my mother, of anyone from Sourwood really, associating themselves with Finneas Ransom is rather ridiculous."

"It is?" I ask before blowing some cool air on my cup of tea. It's still steaming hot.

Janet leans forward and pours herself a cup from the teapot. "Before I get started on who Finneas Ransom is, let me answer your question about Matilda Pinesmith. My mother was friends with her in school back before she disappeared. To be honest, for folks around my age, Matilda is more a ghost story than a missing person, so most of what I know about her is just silly hearsay."

"That's understandable," Harry says.

Janet taps her polished nails against the porcelain of her teacup. "Finneas Ransom is a different story altogether. I suppose, like Matilda, he's a bit of a legend around Sourwood, but not for the same reasons. He owned several large plots of land all throughout the town and had a reputation of sorts." Janet lowers her voice. "When I was a child, the rumor was that anyone who dared to venture onto any of his properties would vanish. Kids liked to say he held people captive. No one knew where the rumors came from. He was sort of the Sourwood boogie man."

I process what Janet has told us. It sounds like somehow over time, Finneas Ransom's connection to Matilda's disappearance morphed itself into a myth about him kidnapping people. My guess is that Janet and her friends never bothered to ask their parents for more information about Finneas Ransom, and instead, let the rumor grow into a local legend among the younger generations.

"What happened to him?" I ask. I know Harry told me Finneas died many years ago, but I wonder if Janet might have more information.

Janet takes a long sip of her tea. "He died when I was in my twenties. He owned about half of Sourwood, and I think he had a couple of kids who inherited the land and then sold it off. He had an oddball wife who never left their house and who had been born and raised deep in the mountains. The Ransom kids were all way older than me, so I can't tell you anything about them, but I imagine they all fled Sourwood as soon as they could. Not much point in sticking around here if you're a Ransom."

The front door to the bakery opens, and the librarian enters, her arms full of thick books. She gives Harry and I a friendly nod.

"I better get back to work," Janet stands up and pushes in her chair as the bakery door opens again.

This time, Eleanor from the card club appears. She is wearing a pretty, blue sweater and has her pearls looped delicately around her aging neck.

"Perfect timing!" Janet says to us and puts a comfortable arm around Eleanor's shoulder. "This is my mother, Eleanor. They used to call her Ella."

CHAPTER THIRTY-SIX

ELLA REVEALS ALL

E leanor wears a confused expression on her face. In habit, she turns one of the pearls on her necklace between her thumb and forefinger over and over again.

"I better run," Janet nods to the back of the bakery where the librarian bends over and examines a Danish filled with colorful jam. She leaves Harry and I sitting at the table with Eleanor standing nearby.

"It's nice to see you two again," Eleanor says awkwardly. "I can't think of the last time I was called Ella." A small flush tickles her pale cheeks. Eleanor takes a step closer to our table and places a hand on the chair Janet recently vacated. "It's nice to see you both out and about. I had been wondering about what had happened at Davy's farm since I last saw you. Remember, Dottie had seen a man out in the fields?"

I think back to meeting Eleanor outside of the sheriff's office and her panic when she told us that Dottie had stopped by Davy's farm only to see a stranger wandering the property. So much has been revealed since that time that it's hard to believe that only a few days have passed.

"You did the right thing by telling us about what Dottie saw," Harry says. "Would you like to have breakfast with us?"

Eleanor hesitates for a moment before shuffling into the empty seat. "Do you mind if I pour myself a cup?" She gestures to the teapot. Next to it, one empty saucer and cup sits.

Harry puts the fine porcelain set in front of Eleanor and pours her some tea. Eleanor adds a large helping of cream and sugar to it.

"Janet opened up this bakery only a few years ago," Eleanor says.

"The food is fantastic," I say and take a bite of my biscuit. I'm considering ordering another one.

"My husband and I were a bit worried about Janet opening it at the time, but I'm glad everything turned out alright." Eleanor stirs some more cream into her tea.

"Why were you worried about your daughter opening the bakery?" I ask. "She's a wonderful baker. I'm starting to think I should've been coming here for my morning breakfast instead of the coffee shop."

Eleanor's lips pinch as she takes a sip of her tea. "We thought that downtown Sourwood would be too competitive for the bakery. Like you said, everyone already goes to the coffee shop. I say, Beatrice is a smart business woman, and I didn't know if our Janet would be able to keep the bakery busy enough."

"The librarian told me that Beatrice owns most of the businesses in town," I say. "I imagine her family has been here a long time like yours then?"

Eleanor twists her pearl necklace so that it lays nicely against her sweater. "Surprisingly, no. Beatrice is rather young, and she only starting buying up properties in Sourwood a few years ago. I say, I think she might be from a big city."

I take a big gulp of tea, hiding my surprise. I had figured that most everyone who lived in Sourwood had probably been born here or nearby.

While the town is quaint and charming, it seems an odd choice for the setting of a business venture by an outsider.

"Eleanor, Emma and I were hoping we could talk to you about the Pinesmith family," Harry says, changing the subject.

"Is this about me telling you about Dottie seeing someone on Davy's property?"

"Actually, we were more interested in your relationship with Matilda Pinesmith," Harry says.

Eleanor's thin hand clasps at her pearls so tightly that her knuckles turn white.

"Our understanding is that you were a close friend to her when she was younger," Harry says kindly.

Eleanor twists her lips and pats down her hair with the hand not attached to her necklace. "We were best friends when we were in school, but I was foolish. I caught a crush on her boyfriend at the time, and we went out behind her back. It wasn't long until she found out. About a year later, she disappeared." Eleanor takes a tissue out of her purse and dabs at the spots under her eyes. "I don't talk about it much."

Eleanor's eyes turn dreamy and a misty layer of glaze settles on them. "I still remember hearing about what happened the day after she went missing. I say, I was so upset. I remember I locked myself in my room and didn't eat hardly anything for weeks."

I reach over and give Eleanor's hand a comforting squeeze. It's been decades since Matilda disappeared, but it's obvious that Eleanor has never let their friendship go. I wonder how she would react if she were to learn that Matilda had been just over the mountain for all this time.

"So, you and Matilda weren't close friends when she disappeared?" Harry asks.

Eleanor's hand tenses under mine. "The opposite in fact. We were closer than ever when she went missing."

Harry raises his eyebrows.

"Wasn't she mad about what happened between you and Finneas Ransom, her boyfriend?" I ask. I have a hard time thinking that I would be okay with one of my friends cuddling up to Harry. Even the thought makes my stomach churn.

"She *was* mad," Eleanor says, "but by the time she disappeared, a year had passed since then. So much had happened. We had graduated from school, I had started a job in town, and Matilda's brother, Davy, was one of the most popular singers in the country. We had left what had happened in the past."

"That must've been hard for her to do," I reply.

Eleanor takes another sip of tea and sets her cup down on its saucer. The little painted flowers on the white porcelain are scratched near the handle where countless hands have worn down the paint over the years. "I don't think it was as hard as some people might think."

Harry tilts his head to the side. This wasn't exactly the answer we'd been expecting.

Eleanor's eyes catch the librarian making herself comfortable in a seat not too far from our table. She lowers her voice so that only Harry and I can hear, "Finneas Ransom was a rotten man, and it wasn't until after Matilda stopped going with him that she finally told me all about his tricks and schemes."

Eleanor takes a deep breath and closes her eyes. A deep line appears across her forehead. Whatever she is about to say must be painful. "When we were in school, Finneas was the most handsome boy. He was athletic and smart. A lot of people in Sourwood thought the world of him, but he thought the world of himself too. I didn't realize it then, but he didn't treat Matilda right.

"He would tell her how to dress, who she could be friends with, even what to eat at lunch. Matilda was so enraptured with him being the most popular boy at school that she acted as if his controlling behavior didn't bother her. Every girl in school wanted to be seen on the arm of Finneas Ransom. Even I did.

"After Matilda caught the two of us kissing, it was like the spell he had cast over her broke. She dumped him that very night. I don't think he had ever been rejected by a girl. Suddenly, all the things that had once made him so appealing faded away. His grades slipped in school, he was kicked off the track team for failing to come to practice, and before he knew it, some other boy in our grade was the new king of the school."

Eleanor traces the pearls on her necklace slowly with her index finger. A look of relief flashes across her face. Telling us the story must have lessened the load she's carried for all these years.

"What happened to Finneas Ransom after the three of you graduated?" I ask while popping the last piece of honeyed biscuit into my mouth. "Your daughter said he became sort of a local legend, but not for the right reasons."

Eleanor takes a moment to respond. "Directly after high school not much happened. I say, I think he worked on a farm somewhere. It wasn't until Matilda went missing that people started thinking about him again, but it certainly wasn't in a good way. He was the number one suspect when she disappeared, but he was cleared of the crime." Eleanor pauses and stares at her tea for a long moment. "I suppose it didn't matter though. His reputation was already ruined by then. Every person in Sourwood with a pulse thought he had something to do with Matilda disappearing."

The honey that tasted so nice moments ago now feels acidic in my mouth. The town of Sourwood had essentially made Finneas Ransom an outcast for a crime he had never committed. For all the years his reputation was ruined, Matilda had been just on the other side of the mountain. I wonder how the people of Sourwood would have treated Finneas Ransom had they known the truth.

The librarian sitting nearby us finishes her morning coffee and pushes in her chair. She gives Harry and I a friendly wave as she leaves the bakery with her stack of books.

"I should be going too," Eleanor says. "I have a couple of errands to run today."

"We really appreciate you talking with us," Harry says.

Eleanor nods her head politely and orders a loaf of bread from her daughter at the counter before heading out. Harry and I sit quietly in the bakery, the smells of raisins and cinnamon swirling around us. I wonder if Matilda knows that her abrupt disappearance led to so much turmoil for Finneas Ransom. Surely Davy or her brother Patrick would have told her? But Davy went on to travel the country right after Matilda's disappearance, so maybe he never really knew what had happened to Finneas Ransom's reputation. And Patrick had left Sourwood and never came back once he was older. How would either of them have known what happened to Finneas?

I turn to look at Harry who is staring out the window, watching a young mother push her child in a purple stroller. The freckles that dot his cheeks and nose contrast with his pale skin in the morning sunlight.

"Should we have told Eleanor that Matilda is alive?" I whisper despite the emptiness of the bakery.

Harry's shoulders rise slightly. "I have no idea."

"It makes me wonder," I say. "Davy and Patrick knew Matilda was in hiding, but I wonder about their parents."

"It's something we could ask Davy," Harry says. "Or Matilda."

Harry reaches across the table and grabs my hand so that he can hold mine in his. "Are you doing okay with all of this?"

I'm a bit thrown by Harry's concern. This isn't the first time that we've been faced with a few twisted stories. Why would this instant be the one where Harry is concerned?

"It's overwhelming, but it's nothing I can't handle with you."

Harry gives me a small kiss on the cheek. "I know, but this time is different. Whatever happened to Ken Kitson is much messier than anything we've ever dealt with before." Harry gives my hand a tight squeeze. "Plus, I know you're not too happy about Davy not showing up to your interview."

Before I have a chance to answer Harry, a face looms in the window of the Bakery. An older man, dressed in torn overalls and with dirt smudged across his leathery face peers through the window until he locks eyes with me. It's Davy Pinesmith, and he looks a mess.

Chapter Thirty-Seven

An Arrest

Davy yanks open the bakery door and stumbles inside. A silver shadow of a beard covers his chin, and he smells musty. It looks like he might've slept in the crawl space under his house.

Harry springs out of his seat to greet Davy. "What happened? Are you okay?"

Davy stares at the counter filled with pastries and fresh bread, but Janet has gone to the back so that it's just Harry and I left in the bakery.

"It's Matilda," he says, spittle collecting at the edge of his lips.

"Is she alright?" I'm now standing too.

"She's as okay as she could be given the circumstances," Davy replies. "Yesterday morning the police showed up to her house and arrested her!"

"What for?" I stand and join Harry.

"The murder of Ken Kitson."

My mouth slides open. Matilda may be guilty of a lot of things, but the idea of the delicate, owl-like woman killing Ken Kitson by attacking him from behind in a deserted field at night doesn't seem plausible.

"How is that possible?" I ask.

"It's not," Davy replies. "She was busy at some potluck of some sort around that time. She couldn't have been two places at once."

"Wait," Harry takes a step forward. "How did you know that Emma and I found out about Matilda?"

A line of suspicion threads its way between Harry's eyes. I had been so caught up in the news that Matilda had been arrested that I hadn't paused to wonder how Davy even knew that we were aware that Matilda was alive.

Davy grunts. "You think I don't talk to my sister? I call her every day."

Harry nods quietly. There's nothing to the simple explanation other than the truth. The way Davy spits out his words shows me that he isn't in the business of making up a lie about something as mundane as speaking with his sister on the phone.

"What information did they have that allowed them to arrest her?" Harry asks, bringing the subject into focus.

"The tread of her shoes matched prints found near Ken Kitson. The police received an anonymous call from someone suggesting that Matilda's shoes be investigated." Thick lines dredge their way across Davy's forehead. "But Matilda is innocent. Like I said, Matilda wouldn't have been anywhere near Ken Kitson when he was killed."

Harry and I exchange a knowing look. Matilda's shoes matching what was found at the crime scene isn't something to overlook, but the fact that the information came from an anonymous phone call is suspicious. It sounds like too much of a coincidence.

"We need to get the sheriff and head over the mountain. She's being held over there since there's nowhere to hold people in Sourwood." Davy doesn't wait for Harry and I to reply. He's out and back on the sidewalk just as quickly as he appeared in the bakery.

Harry and I gather our things and rush after him, spotting him on his way down the street. It's not long before he disappears into the sheriff's office. Harry hops around a group of older hikers blocking the sidewalk while I skip over a small flowerpot as we make our way towards the sheriff's. Sourwood is the most crowded that I've ever seen it. I barely avoid tumbling into the roadway as I dart around a dog walker and a group of rambunctious golden retrievers while Harry sprints ahead. Finally, we make it to the sheriff's office in one piece. Inside, Davy is standing at the desk, fuming. The scene is reminiscent of the first time that we were in th e office, and Davy was filing a report about someone stealing his goat.

"What do you mean you haven't heard anything?" Davy's mouth is taut. "This desk is a mess. I'm not surprised that you can't keep track of anything in here!"

"There's no messages on the phone. Anyways, are you sure that she was taken to the station?" the sheriff asks.

"What, you think I was dreaming?" Davy scoffs.

Harry bends down on the floor and holds up a long phone cable. The blue tip of the cord shines in the light. "I think I may have found the problem with the phone," Harry says.

Davy lets out a gruff sound from deep in his throat.

"I was wondering what that was for," the sheriff itches a spot on his head.

"We need to get going," Davy insists, an air of impatience slipping into his voice. "The faster we can get over the mountain, the better. We need to get Matilda released." Davy takes out an envelope from his back pocket. It's thin and has loopy handwriting on it. "Matilda wrote down the numbers of everyone at the potluck who can swear that she was there. It was some sort of youth lock-in that she was chaperoning at the church, so she was there from sunset to sunrise. It would have been impossible for her to be anywhere near Ken Kitson that night."

The sheriff gets to his feet and grabs a pair of keys hanging near his desk. I guess his wife has decided that he's well enough to drive again. At least, I hope he is. The mountain roads are winding and dangerous.

"The cruiser is just outside. We'll get Matilda out in a jiffy," he strides out onto the sidewalk, not an ounce of concern dimming his steps.

Davy huffs and shakes his head. "The two of you better come along. I don't want Melville messing anything up."

CHAPTER THIRTY-EIGHT

AN INTERVIEW AT LAST

T he foam from my steaming latte slips over the edge of the mug that the barista sets in front of me. Harry ordered his coffee black while Davy, surprisingly, went with something called a lemon-mint balm tea. While the smell of freshly brewed coffee tops my list of favorite things, the aroma seeping into the air from Davy's morning tea is delectable.

The sheriff dropped Harry, Davy, and I off at a tiny coffee shop two towns over from the police station where Matilda is being held. He let us know that he might be gone for a bit while he established Matilda's alibi and got her out. The shop itself is similar to Country Time Coffee. It has the same cozy atmosphere with local art decorating the walls and warm colors accenting the room.

The three of us are quiet as we watch a small group of goldfinches fly around the weedy parking lot. One of the male birds is particularly bright with yellow feathers that shine in the sun. The little scene, as pleasing as it is, drives a stake through my chest. I've been ignoring Mr. Hawking's calls and texts. There's only so much time before he calls me up to tell me I no longer have a job.

"A group of them is called a charm," Davy's gruff voice interrupts my thoughts.

"Sorry, what did you say?" I blink back into reality.

"A group of goldfinches is called a charm," Davy repeats. "A group of crows is a murder, and a group of ravens is an unkindness." Davy's eyes stare out the window as he watches a goldfinch dance in the air. "I know I haven't been too kind to you these past few days. I owe you an apology for standing you up for our interview," Davy says. "I like to think of myself as a man of my word."

A bit of my latte splashes onto the tabletop as I roughly set my cup down. The milky brown liquid looks like it has morphed into the shape of a bird. Or maybe my mind just can't stop thinking about the fact that Davy just apologized to me after spewing out a list of bird facts.

"It's okay," the words stumble out. "There was an emergency with your sister."

Davy's apology doesn't feel real. Who is this usually gruff but sometimes sensitive man? His eyes look almost kind as they follow a pair of goldfinches hover over a grassy patch outside. I still can't find it in me to completely trust him though. As much as I want to believe that it isn't possible, what if Davy is the reason Ken Kitson is dead?

Davy doesn't look away from the tiny finches in the parking lot. "I should've put in a call to the coffee shop so that Beatrice could've told you where I was."

"You could give her the interview now," Harry pipes up. "Sheriff Melville said it would be a while before he comes back, so you might as well."

Davy is silent, and for a moment, I think he's going to tell Harry off, but then the older man shifts in his seat so that he's facing me. His eyes are digging into mine.

"I would like that. I want my fans to know what I've been up to all these years," he says.

"That would be amazing. Thank you so much." I paste on a smile.

I don't have a notebook or my laptop with me, but I can't let this opportunity fade. I may never get the chance again. I'll just have to pay attention and remember the facts. Later, I can send Davy a write-up for him to approve. A small voice in my head whispers that I might not have that opportunity if it turns out Davy was the one who hurt Ken Kitson, but I shoo that voice away. I can't let possibilities jump in the path of something that might make or break my career.

"I haven't been interviewed in some time." Davy clears his throat. "In my younger years, the reporters were pushy when it came to getting the story they wanted, but this time I want to do things different. I'll tell you my story, but I'm doing it my way."

"I wouldn't expect anything less," I lean back and relax my arms. I have a hard time envisioning anyone pushing Davy around.

"I'll get started then." Davy places his weathered hands on the table. Underneath his short nails, black dirt paints his skin, a testament to his time spent in the outdoors.

"When the time came for me to put music behind me and settle into a quieter life, I had no doubt that I would come back to the farm near Goldfinch Gap. I knew my parents wanted to retire to an area that would be warmer throughout the year, so I offered to buy the farmhouse and a large part of the property from them. They wouldn't accept my money at first, but eventually, they gave in as my father grew ill. I didn't buy all the land. Some of it remained deeded to them so that Patrick would inherit something when they passed. As you know, the land that Ken Kitson was found on was owned by Patrick and not me. I just kept it up for him for all these years."

Davy takes a long sip of his tea. "For the first few years, I toiled on the land like my father had, but I soon grew tired of that. After a while, I got the idea to transform the farm. I know it doesn't look like much but empty fields and patches of forest, but that was my goal.

"Not long after I moved back to Sourwood, I learned that the American goldfinches that that had patterned the landscape of Sourwood for years were diminishing, and no one knew why. I researched and learned that across the country, the finches weren't endangered and were considered a healthy species, so what was happening in Sourwood? How could we be the town of the famous Goldfinch Gap, and there be no more goldfinches?

"I educated myself and decided I would do what I could to bring the little birds back to Sourwood. I spent years planting thistle that had once been native to the area but squeezed out due to the farming. I undammed some of the old creek points my own father had stopped up and rerouted them so that the fields would flood more. Soon, the little yellow birds started reappearing."

Davy's story paints pictures in my head of green fields dotted with little birds the color of the sun. I don't blame him for wanting to keep the goldfinch population in Sourwood healthy. There are few birds that are as majestic as the American goldfinch.

"And that's the story." Davy drains the rest of the tea. "Probably not what you were expecting, but it's short and to the point, and most importantly, it's true."

"I know it's not relevant to the story, but did your sister, Matilda, get any land?" Harry asks.

Davy hesitates. "My parents didn't know where Matilda went at first. Matilda didn't want either me or Patrick telling them about what had happened, but eventually, telling them was the right thing to do. They never told a soul where she went." Davy takes a long look out the window. "When they passed, they left her out of the will. They were a bit hurt about her leaving."

The door to the shop opens and the sheriff appears. He catches our eyes and slowly makes his way to our table. I've never seen him look so glum. Even in the hospital, his cheeks had a bit of rosiness to them. He plops down into the seat next to Davy.

"That took a while," he grabs a menu off the table. "Matilda is safe and sound back at her house. We made several calls and home visits, and multiple people confirmed she had been at the church all night. The reverend was most adamant about it."

The sheriff drops the menu and looks at the three of us with an intense stare. "Anyways, I'm sorry to say it Davy, but it looks like someone set up your sister."

Chapter Thirty-Nine

Old Friends Come to Light

The sheriff adds a packet of sugar to his coffee. The small crystals disappear beneath the thick, brown liquid as he stirs the drink.

"I have to be good about watching my sugar levels after I fainted and went to the hospital," the sheriff says to me. "Anyways, if I end up in the hospital again, Polly says she'll make me retire, and I can't have that happen. Then, I would have to sit at home with her all day."

"Let us know if you need anything," Harry says. "We don't want anything to happen to you now that you feel better."

The sheriff takes a long sip from his mug. "Believe me, I don't want to pass out again. Polly has it in her head that I might be going loopy because when they took me to the hospital, they asked me when I had last had something to help with my blood levels, and I told them the last thing I did before blacking out was have a nice cup of coffee with some sugar at Country Time Coffee." The sheriff shrugs his broad shoulders. "I must've been so busy that day that I thought I had my coffee break when I didn't. A bit embarrassing."

Davy's eyes watch the sheriff intently. There's a long pause of silence, indicating the end of the conversation.

"So, about Matilda," Davy says. "You said she's being set up?"

"Unfortunately, that's the fact. This is the second time now that someone has tried, and failed, to link her to the murder of Ken Kitson on your brother's property."

Davy contorts his face into a scowl. "Who would do that though? Matilda minds only her business. No one would be out there to bother her."

One of the goldfinches outside flies by the window at the same time as a new idea flutters to mind. While Davy isn't wrong about Matilda keeping to herself, he's wrong to think that no one might have something against her. What if someone had found out about Matilda the same way that Harry had and felt betrayed at her disappearance? Finneas Ransom is long gone, but there was someone in Sourwood who might have felt slighted had they learned the truth about Matilda.

Eleanor had been Matilda's best friend. Based on what Harry and I had seen of her, she was a sensitive woman. Who is to say that she didn't happen upon Matilda in one way or another? Eleanor could've felt resentment at having grieved her friend for most of her life only for Matilda to be alive and well on the other side of the mountain.

I try to catch Harry's eye to give him some kind of signal that I need to speak with him urgently, but he's wrapped up in a story the sheriff is telling that's unrelated to the case. I mumble something about needing another latte so that I can leave the table. I need a moment by myself. Sitting at the table feels stagnant, and my thoughts are jumbled in my head.

I order a latte to-go at the counter of the coffee shop before taking a step outside. The flock of goldfinches has gone, and it's just me in the parking lot with a lone crow.

If Eleanor is guilty of trying to frame Matilda for the murder of Ken Kitson, does that mean she is guilty of killing him too? And if so, how would she even have done it? There's no way that she would've been able to overtake a full-grown man considering her height and stature. Could she have asked her daughter to do it for her? No, her daughter didn't even know her mother had ever dated Finneas Ransom and been associated with Matilda. Plus, Eleanor had been extremely helpful. She had given Harry and I plenty of leads these past few days. She wouldn't do that if she had been the one to kill Ken Kitson.

Still, it didn't rule out the possibility that she had been the one anonymously leaving tips about Matilda. Eleanor could have nothing to do with Ken Kitson and still have decided to try and make Matilda's life difficult.

A light breeze causes a few blossoms to slowly drift to the ground. I go back inside and stop by the counter to pick up my latte. I take a small taste to check that it's correct.

"Is everything good?" the girl behind the counter asks.

"Perfect," I say. "There's actually a coffee shop on the other side of the mountain that makes a latte just like this. When I head back home, I'm going to miss my morning coffees."

"Is it Country Time Coffee?" the girl asks.

"That's the one," I reply before taking another sip.

"We're actually owned by the same person," the girl says.

"Beatrice owns this place too?"

The girl nods her head. "The same one. She opened this one about five months ago. I think it's her first business outside of Sourwood. She stops in once and a while, especially on Sundays. That's when we have big church-going crowds."

An elderly couple comes through the door, and I excuse myself so that the girl can greet them. For such a small area, Beatrice has managed to build an empire. She must have a lot of business smarts.

When I return to the table, the sheriff is standing up and Davy and Harry are shrugging into their light jackets. Davy looks miserable, but that tends to be the default look he wears on his face. The sheriff gives me a cheerful smile when he sees that I've ordered a drink to-go.

"It looks like we're all set," the sheriff says.

"Where will we go when we get back to Sourwood?" I ask.

"Not too sure about that," the sheriff replies. "While you were grabbing your drink, the three of us had a little discussion, and it was determined that we weren't going back to Sourwood just yet." The sheriff eyes Davy.

Harry wraps his arm around my back and gives my shoulder a gentle squeeze. "We're going to stop by Matilda's and have a private chat. Right, Davy?"

Davy doesn't respond. He strides out of the coffee shop.

"What's going on?" I ask.

Harry watches Davy pace in the parking lot. "He's mad. The sheriff and I finally teamed up and confronted him. We told him that Matilda's story just doesn't add up. He tried defending it at first, but he crumbled. He said he would go over to her house with us and encourage Matilda to tell the truth since it might be the only way to protect her from being framed again."

"You two coming?" the sheriff calls from where he holds the door to the coffee shop open.

"We're on your heels," Harry says.

I follow the men out of the shop and into the car. I hope we're all headed in the direction of the truth.

CHAPTER FORTY

A FAMILY TALE

The orange cat lays on its back and paws at the lacy edge of the doily hanging off of Matilda's coffee table. Davy, the sheriff, Harry, and I all sit in Matilda's living room while she busies herself with a plate of cookies in the kitchen. As far as she's aware, we've all stopped by for a short check-in after she was held in jail overnight.

"What do you think is the best way to go about getting her to tell us the truth?" Harry whispers in my ear. The two of us are on the couch together while Davy and the sheriff sit in chairs in corners on the opposite side of the room.

"I don't think we should let Davy take the lead," I say back, lowering my voice so the older men can't hear. "He might lie."

Harry nods his head.

"Let me take the lead," I say. "I have an idea."

Matilda bustles out of the kitchen holding a silver tray stacked with shortbread cookies. She sets it on the center table before taking a seat next to me on the sofa. She looks tired with sunken, half-moons under her eyes and her hair frizzing out on the ends.

"How are you doing?" I ask her gently.

She takes a deep breath. "Much better now that Sheriff Melville helped me get out of that holding cell. I can't think of anyone in the world who would accuse me of a crime like murder, let alone set me up." Her voice breaks at the end of her sentence.

"Matilda," I place a soft hand on her shoulder, "do you think you could share with us the real reason you disappeared all those years ago with the help of your brothers? I know it seems ages ago, but when someone is this determined to frame you for murder, it's important that we examine everyone you ever could've offended."

Matilda exchanges a look with Davy across the room. I can't make out what it means, but it appears as if the two are in agreement.

Davy leans forward and rests his elbows on his knees. His arms are thin but muscular from years of work on the farm. "It's time."

Matilda picks at the cloth of her skirt. The nostrils on her long nose flair, and her owl eyes droop in a look of defeat. "As you might have already guessed, I didn't disappear from Sourwood to avoid the embarrassment that came with the end of my relationship with Finneas Ransom. Quite the opposite actually. I ran away because Finneas Ransom was going to kill me."

The room is silent except for the loud meows of the orange cat on the floor.

"Could you explain a bit more?" Harry asks.

Matilda's face turns pale and her eyes water.

"I'll do it," Davy speaks up, taking the heat away from his sister. "Finneas Ransom was the biggest pest Sourwood ever saw. My brother and I never took a liking to him with the way he treated her. When the two of them were going together, he told her how to dress and how to behave, but the real trouble came after Matilda dumped him.

"Matilda had caught Finneas with her friend and told him they were done. Patrick and I were happy for her, and the whole family thought that we had seen the last of Finneas Ransom, but we were wrong. He started sneaking over to the house at night, doing odd things. At first it was the type of things young men do when they're heartbroken. He would leave letters in the mailbox and flowers on the porch, but soon things turned dark.

"My mother was the first one to catch him one night peering through the window as we ate family dinner. Soon, Patrick found him in one of the fields. Finneas had binoculars with him and had been spying on Matilda as she worked in the garden. Finneas ran both times he was discovered.

"Then one night, he showed up to the farm while I was alone. The rest of the family had gone out somewhere. My old brain can't recall where, but I know I was alone. Finneas banged on the front door like a ghost was after him. I opened it, and it was clear the man had been drinking. He smelt and his eyes were glazed over. He grabbed me by the shirt collar and threw me against the doorframe. He told me that if Matilda didn't come back to him, he would kill her so that no other man could have her.

"The two of us had a scuffle on the porch until Finneas beat a hasty retreat. I thought that was the end of it. Some men can't handle their liquor, and I figured Finneas wouldn't even remember what he had done in the morning, so I didn't bother Matilda about what happened. I didn't want to upset her."

Davy takes a measured breath as he stares down at his tanned arms. "That would turn out to be a mistake. Not long after the incident on the porch, Finneas came back, but this time, he hadn't come to deliver a warning, he had come to kill Matilda."

The orange cat brushes up against Davy's trousers, and he pauses to pet the cat for a short second. Whatever he is building up to must be difficult to say.

Davy gives the cat a firm pat, and it saunters away. "I wasn't meant to be home the night that Finneas came to kill Matilda. I had been scheduled to play a concert at a college a couple hours away, but the school had canceled last minute. I had gone to my room early in the night to work on some songs. While I was sitting on my bed with my journal, I heard Matilda scream.

"I jumped up and went into her room and found Finneas. He had a gun pointed at her, and he looked ready to fire. I didn't think. I tackled Finneas to the ground. The two of us struggled, and eventually, Patrick came in. Patrick and I managed to overpower him and knock him out with the butt of his gun."

Davy rubs his forehead. "It was on that night we realized that Matilda had to leave Sourwood, and she had to leave in a way that would get Finneas to stop looking for her. Patrick and I dragged Finneas down the road and laid him in a ditch with a half-empty bottle of whiskey we took from our father's liquor cabinet. We hoped he would wake up and be none the wiser as to how he ended up there. Unlike the night where we had scuffled on the porch, on this night he had taken a hit to the head, so we crossed our fingers that he might not remember everything.

"When we got back to the house, we helped Matilda get to the trails near Goldfinch Gap. The three of us had spent our whole childhood on the trails, and we knew our way around the forest better than anyone in Sourwood. Matilda made her way to the other side of the mountain to stay with an old girlfriend of mine.

"You see, back in that day, I was something of a teenage heartthrob, so the media would hound any young lady they thought I had ever taken out on a date. This old girlfriend in particular knew how to keep quiet if anyone came around asking questions, including police. I knew Matilda would be safe with her, and she was.

"Once Patrick and I felt that Matilda was finally out of harm's way, we called in the kidnapping and told some story to the sheriff's office. They looked into Finneas for a second, but soon, the town of Sourwood moved on, and so did our family and Matilda. We were finally at peace, and we had been up until the murder of Ken Kitson just a few weeks ago."

"Is all this true?" Harry asks Matilda.

The woman tenses. "It is. I'll never forget it. I was sitting at my vanity table, taking off my day's makeup, when I saw a shadow in the mirror. I turned around, and Finneas Ransom was standing in my bedroom with a gun. I screamed. I thought for sure that image would be the last thing I ever saw. If it hadn't been for Davy," she looks over at her brother, "I might not be sitting here today."

"What I don't understand is why didn't you ever tell me any of this?" the sheriff asks. "I was working at the department when all this happened. Anyways, I would've helped. I wouldn't have let someone like Finneas get away with stalking Matilda and threatening her." A look of hurt takes over the sheriff's face, causing his bushy eyebrows to turn down.

"I think your memory is growing watery," Davy says. "You did work for the station back then, but you weren't in charge. Don't you remember who the sheriff was when you were a deputy?"

The sheriff's mouth drops open. "I had completely forgotten."

The sheriff turns away from Davy so that his shoulders are facing the couch where Harry and I sit. "I had led the investigation into Matilda's disappearance all those years ago like I told the two of you, but it wasn't because I was the town's sheriff. It was because the sheriff at the time, my boss, was Lance Ransom, Finneas Ransom's father. He couldn't lead the case since his own son was a suspect." The sheriff turns back to Davy. "And I'm guessing Lance Ransom was the reason you felt like you had to hide Matilda away instead of getting help?"

Davy shrugs his shoulders. "Now that I've gained a bit of understanding about the world, I realize that what Patrick, Matilda and I did wasn't the best choice, or even the right choice, but by the time we came to that conclusion, it was too late. We didn't want to get in trouble for staging the kidnapping. And the way we saw it, no one got hurt. Our parents knew what happened and grew to accept it, and Finneas Ransom lived his life."

"That's the story," Matilda stops pulling at the loose string on her skirt. "I'll be honest, I thought I would feel differently if anyone ever found out the truth, like a weight had been lifted from my shoulders, but I feel the opposite."

"It's probably from the stress of spending a night in jail," Harry says.

Matilda scoops up her orange cat and gives it a cuddle. "My story doesn't help us figure out why someone would frame me. The only person in that story who would want to hurt me would be Finneas Ransom, and he's long gone."

Matilda is right. Harry and I had been thinking that if we could just get the truth out of Matilda, then we would be able to understand what had happened to Ken Kitson, but it really does look like the two crimes have nothing to do with one another.

The cat snuggles its head under Matilda's chin and lets out a loud purr. At least somebody in the room is happy.

CHAPTER FORTY-ONE
PACKING UP

My computer dings as the email containing my interview with Davy flies away to Mr. Hawking's inbox. I know Mr. Hawking won't be pleased with how late my article is delivered, but he can't be too mad. I did get his magazine the interview of a lifetime.

When we got back in town, I asked the sheriff if he could drop me off at the cabin so that I could have some time to work on my writing. Harry had insisted that I go back to Charlie's place instead of mine. He was worried that my cabin wouldn't be safe after last night, but I told him I needed a place to concentrate on my writing. Charlie's cabin made it too easy for me to slip into conversation with Harry, so I had to be alone. Plus, in the daylight, the cabin didn't seem as daunting as it had the previous night.

It had been a good choice too considering how quickly I had been able to polish off the article. Writing down everything that Davy told me as soon as I could prevented me from forgetting all the facts. With hearing both Davy's story and Matilda's story so close together, I couldn't take the risk of mixing up the details.

I turn my computer off just as my phone buzzes. It's probably Mr. Hawking already. He has the uncanny ability to know whenever I send an email.

I glance down at my phone, and I'm surprised to see a missed call from an unfamiliar number. I call the number back and wait as the phone buzzes.

"Hello, Sourwood Sheriff's office," the sheriff sounds a bit nasally on the phone, a surprise considering his voice usually isn't.

"It's me, Emma Finch. I have a missed call from you," I say.

"Yes, Emma! I'm so happy you called back. I have some bad news."

My heart trembles in my chest. What could have happened? Did someone hurt Matilda? Or did another person turn up dead near Davy's farm?

"What happened?"

"We were so busy today that I forgot to tell you that the rental on the cabin is up this afternoon. You'll need to leave by four. I tried to get you a few more days, but it turns out the place is booked solid for the next few weeks. Anyways, a warm front is moving in, and a lot of hikers are coming out to Sourwood so that they can climb the trails near Goldfinch Gap."

I'm part relieved and part panicked. Nothing bad has happened, but I need to get my things together if I'm going to be out of the cabin by four. A glance at the kitchen clock shows I only have half an hour.

"Polly said she could put the spare room together for you," the sheriff says, "but I'm not sure if that would be the best idea. Polly likes crafts, and our spare room is filled with scrapbooking knickknacks."

"That's a kind offer, but I think I'll pass," I say. The thought of sharing a bed with boxes of glitter and double-sided tape isn't exactly tempting. Plus, Charlie has his big cabin rental. He could lend me the room I used last night.

"Give me a ring if you change your mind," the sheriff hangs up the phone.

I don't waste much time stuffing my clothes into the suitcase. Thankfully, I hadn't packed much and a lot of my things are already at Charlie's. By the time everything is squared away and I've double checked that nothing is left in the cabin, I head out the front door right at four o'clock. As I close the door, the electronic lock clicks behind me. The owner of the cabin must've been able to reset it through some sort of virtual program.

I take a step onto the gravel driveway and head over to my car when realization hits me. I still don't have the correct key. How am I going to get anywhere without a car? Not only that, but how am I going to get my car moved out of the driveway? All the excitement that had filled me minutes ago when I had finished my article slowly trickles away.

I grab my phone and dial Charlie. I hope he's willing to take a break from searching for his cheese to help me out. Other than the sheriff and Davy, he's the only one I know in Sourwood with a vehicle.

On the last ring, Charlie picks up.

"Charlie, do you think you could help me out?"

There's banging noises in the background. "Not at this exact time. Is everything alright?"

"The rental on the cabin is up, and I was hoping I could crash at your place tonight?"

The clanging in the background stops, and I can hear Harry ask *what did she say?* To Charlie on the other side of the line.

"Emma, you won't be too pleased to hear this, but Harry and I are running around like escaped chickens because we also need to be out of my cabin in an hour. I became so caught up with finding that cheese and helping you two solve that murder, that I forgot that I had only reserved the cabin until today." Charlie makes a clicking sound with his tongue. "Harry was just about to call and ask if we could sleep at your place."

"I can't believe this timing. What are we going to do?"

"We'll figure something out," Charlie says. "I have to let you go now. Harry and I need to hurry up if we're going to be out of the cabin in time."

I put my phone away and take a seat on the front steps. At least the weather is nice. There's a light breeze, and it's early enough in the spring season that insects and other bugs aren't out biting. I'll call Charlie or Harry back in a bit so that they have more time to pack their things.

A crack comes from the woods, and I squint my eyes to better see into the dark forest. Ivy covers sections of the ground like a patterned rug, and twisted roots disappear below ground. A gray squirrel sits at the base of a nearby tree, nibbling on an acorn. I don't know what I would do if someone were to be watching me from the woods. I'm in the open without a car or cabin to flee to.

My phone buzzes, but it's not Charlie or Harry. It's just a text from Mr. Hawking saying that he got the article and that I should take the rest of the week off as a reward for my hard work. My blood should be glowing with happiness, but it's not. All I can think about is getting away from the forest.

From a distance, the sound of an engine breaks the still air. Out on the road, a truck rumbles on its way up the mountain. Whoever is driving must see me standing in the driveway with my luggage because the truck slows as it nears.

The window of the truck rolls down, and the gruff voice of Davy greets me, "What are you doing out here on the side of the road? You're going to get yourself hit!"

"I can't get into my car," heat crawls across my cheeks, "and I can't get back into my cabin since today was the last day of my rental."

Davy looks unimpressed with me. "So, you're planning on sleeping out by the road? That's not the brightest."

"I think I'll stay at the sheriff's," I stutter. Maybe sharing a bed with craft supplies isn't as bad as I had originally thought. A little bit of glue and glitter never hurt anyone.

Davy chortles from his seat in the truck. His laugh is dry and exactly as I imagined it would be. "Have fun with that. Polly has more things stuffed in their guest room than the nearest department store. You'll be lucky to find a place to stand let alone sleep."

"I don't know what to do then."

Davy must read the defeat written across my face because his hard features soften, something I haven't seen before. "I'll tell you what. I have that big farmhouse all to myself. I can fix a bed up for you."

I seem to be unable to push any words out of my mouth. Never would I ever have imagined Davy would let me borrow a room at his house. In fact, not too long ago, I would've thought him to be a prime suspect in the murder of Ken Kitson. But as I peer into his truck, there's no hesitation in my gut. Over the past few days, all I've learned about Davy is that he's a man who deeply cares about his sister, his farm, and his community. Now that I've gotten to know Davy, I realize what the sheriff has been saying about him all along is right. He might be a bit grumpy, but he's not a murderer.

"I can't even tell you how much I would appreciate that."

Davy pushes the passenger door open for me so that I can climb inside the cab. As I'm settling into the seat, my phone buzzes. It's Charlie again.

"We're all packed," he says. "Harry and I will swing by the cabin and pick you up. Maybe there's a hotel somewhere that can take us in for the night."

"I've actually found a place," I say into the phone. "Davy offered me one of the rooms at his house."

"What! You can't stay with him!" Charlie shouts through the receiver.

If Davy heard Charlie, he doesn't show it.

"It's the right choice," I say into the phone, "and I feel good about it in my gut."

"Well, now that you mention your gut, you must be right," Charlie snaps.

There are some raised voices on the end of Charlie's line, and Harry's warm voice comes over the speaker.

"Could you ask Davy if he might consider taking Charlie and I in too? I've been looking for nearby hotels ever since we realized we had to vacate the cabin, and the closest one is almost an hour away."

"I'll ask him. If he agrees, I'll send you a text," I say and hang up.

Davy shifts the gear into drive. "Done dillydallying?"

I buckle myself up. "I was wondering if you would be willing to help Charlie and Harry out too. They also need a place to stay."

"Your lot isn't very organized," Davy grumbles. "Tell them I can make room."

If Davy was the type to receive a hug without thinking it was an invitation to a fistfight, I think I would give him one right now. He has no idea how much of a help he has been today. I type a text out to Harry and lean back in the seat. Maybe everything will be okay tonight.

CHAPTER FORTY-TWO

A LATE SNACK

Davy leans back in his rocking chair and folds his one leg over the other. After Harry and Charlie had arrived at the farmhouse and Davy had shown us all to our rooms, he made a simple dinner of eggs and sausages and served us in the living room since there weren't enough seats in the kitchen to host us all.

Like the kitchen, the living room doesn't have too many decorations. There's a threadbare rug that matches the tan sofa and chairs. Not much is on the wall other than a black and white photograph of a family standing in front of an old barn. I assume the photo is of Davy and his family when he was just a child. Davy bears a resemblance to the man in the picture with his sharp cheek bones and sunken eyes. If it wasn't for the large television in the corner of the room, a person might think they had stepped back in time.

"You three don't need to bother and stay up with me," Davy says. "There's a few shows I like to watch before bed." He presses a button on the remote and the television zaps to life.

"Thank you for the hospitality," Charlie rubs his eyes as he gets to his feet. "I've spent all day hunting down cheese, so I'm off to an early bedtime."

Davy threads his eyebrows together, but if he finds Charlie's comment odd, he doesn't say anything.

Charlie exits the room right as a boom of thunder sounds in the air.

"Never mind," Charlie appears back in the room. "I can stay up a little longer." Another thunderous bang shakes the windows, and Charlie hugs himself as a small shiver run down his arms.

"It's the cold air and the hot air intermingling," Davy rocks back in his chair. "Happens every spring around here. I wouldn't be surprised if this one came with a good bit of rain. I find the ones at night always do in these parts."

Charlie's mouth turns down in a frown, and he returns to the chair he had vacated only seconds ago. I don't blame Charlie for refusing to go upstairs. Davy's house doesn't seem well maintained and while the downstairs seems sturdy, the upstairs is another story. When Davy had shown us to our rooms earlier, mine had a sloping floor and Harry's had a prominent watermark on the ceiling most likely from a longstanding leak.

There's another echoing crash that shakes the house. The lamps dim and the television goes fuzzy. Davy grumbles and clicks the off button on the remote.

"Cable goes out whenever it rains." Davy snorts and looks out the window where the rain runs down as a curtain of water.

For several minutes, the only sounds are of the drops pounding against the ground and the sides of the house. It sounds a bit like static with so much water crashing to the earth at once.

Davy silently stands. "I wouldn't mind a snack. Anyone else?"

I shake my head politely while Harry thanks Davy for the offer, but passes it up. Charlie is the only one to accept.

Once Davy leaves the room, Charlie lets out a loud groan. "I'm not sleeping upstairs until this storm passes. If I go to bed up there, I have a higher chance of being blown away than finding that cheese in town."

"Maybe it will be over quickly. The last storm that went through Sourwood didn't last long," I say in a hushed tone.

"Being blown away isn't even my main concern," Charlie says. "What if Davy killed Ken Kitson, and he's plotting to take care of us next? I'm not sure if you two recall, but I didn't want to stay here in the first place. It was Harry who made me come over here." Charlie gives Harry a hard look not befitting for a man of his age.

Harry turns to me, and that's when it hits me. Charlie hasn't been with us all day, and neither Harry nor I have had a chance to catch him up on everything we've learned. If Harry is having the same thoughts as I am, he no doubt thinks Davy is innocent. After hearing Matilda's story and learning about what Davy and Patrick did to help their sister, I am confident that Davy would never kill a stranger on his property. No, he would never want to risk someone discovering that Matilda was still alive. Even after all these years, he wanted family secrets to stay that way: secret.

I open my mouth to explain to Charlie that Davy isn't dangerous when Davy comes trotting back into the room holding two plates of cheese and crackers. The food isn't the most artistic, but it looks delicious. I regret saying I didn't want an evening snack. I hope Charlie will share.

Davy sits down and places a large chunk of cheese on a cracker. The cheese is a pale white rimmed with some sort of crunchy coating. The smell is pungent yet sweet and reminds me a bit of Christmas.

"Are you okay?" Harry is looking at Charlie.

Charlie has lost all of his coloring. His face is as white as the cheese, and his eyes are wide as they take in the simple spread in front of him.

Charlie delicately lifts the cheese to his nose and takes a whiff. "Is the crust cranberry and apple cinnamon?"

Davy swallows a bite of food. "That's what they tell people," Davy replies. "I know the fellow who makes the stuff. He's just a few farms over. Most people think the secret is the fig that comes in the center of the cheese, but I know the real secret." Davy takes another large bite of cheese and cracker.

"What is it?" Charlie asks as if Davy holds all the knowledge of the world.

"Muscadines," Davy says in his rough voice. "I can't tell you what the fellow does with them, but they're in there all right. It gives the cheese a bit of a rustic tang."

Harry raises his eyebrows, and I exchange a discreet look with him. Davy is the last person on earth I would have imaged using the phrase *rustic tang*. The man truly is a dichotomy.

"You have no idea how long I have been looking for this cheese," Charlie practically sings before carefully placing a morsel in his mouth.

He closes his eyes and is lost for a moment. I can't believe Charlie has spent close to a week looking for this cheese all over Sourwood only for it to be stocked in Davy's refrigerator this whole time. Charlie's eyes flutter back to life before he busies himself with the rest of the cheese on his plate. Davy's own plate clinks against the table as he puts it down. In the time it took Charlie to eat one piece of cheese, Davy has finished his food.

"Davy," Harry readjusts himself on the couch and pushes one of the plain pillows under his back. "I did want to thank you for your help today with Matilda. I know that without you, your sister wouldn't have told us the story about her disappearance."

Davy rubs his nose and snorts. I really don't know how Dottie finds his brutish mannerisms attractive. "We didn't have much choice in the matter. It's like what was said, someone is after Matilda, and we needed to think about anyone and everyone, but Finneas Ransom is dead and gone, so he can't have anything to do with it."

"Based on what Harry and I learned in town earlier while we were in the bakery, Finneas Ransom didn't exactly have a very good reputation around Sourwood in his later years."

Davy is quiet for a moment. I wonder if he's ignoring me when he finally speaks, "Finneas didn't have the easiest time after Matilda's disappearance. He was cleared of the crime, but a lot of people in town didn't trust him anymore. I felt a bit put out about his reputation, knowing that Matilda was alive the whole time. But Patrick, he felt that Davy was as good as a murderer the way he had attacked Matilda. Plus, he worried that if we were to reveal that Matilda was still alive, Finneas would go after her."

"Do you think he would try to hurt her again after all those years? Didn't he end up getting married and having a family?" I ask.

Davy leans back in his chair and his knees let out a crack. "I don't like to say things like this, but something wasn't all the way right with Finneas. In his older years, the kids in town were scared to walk by his house. Rumor had it that he would yell some nasty things at them. It was difficult too because he owned a lot of the land in the town. There was even a fellow I had been in school with who tried to run a butcher's shop on the main street, but Davy was his landlord. The shop wasn't in business for more than half a year. Ransom price-gouged. I don't think Patrick was wrong to keep Matilda safe."

"What about his wife? If he had been so cruel towards Matilda, didn't you ever wonder about the woman he married?" Based on what Davy and Matilda have told me, I can't imagine being married to someone like Finneas. Not only was he controlling, but he could hurt someone whenever something didn't go the way he liked.

Davy pulls his mouth into a lopsided grin. "Bea Ransom wasn't the type of woman people worried about. She was a woman from the mountains. She could take care of herself. I think most of the town was scared of her. If Finneas ever tried anything on her, he'd probably have been shot dead in the forest. She was a legend herself. She had grown up in the woods and her parents were the best hunters around. Rumor was that she'd killed her first bear at eight. Even to this day, I've never seen anyone handle a gun like that woman."

An image of a burly woman with bushy hair and large muscles fills my mind. It's just the type of person who could've hurt Ken Kitson and then set up Matilda as the murderer, but was this Bea Ransom still even alive? And if she was, was she even well enough to do what she did in her younger years?

Harry must be having the same thought because he asks Davy, "Where is Bea Ransom today?"

Davy laughs. "That old witch lives with her daughter on the other side of the country. After Finneas died, she left these parts, and she hasn't been seen around here since. I know Dottie makes a call to her now and then. I think Bea and her are second cousins of sorts. Based on what Dottie says, Bea isn't the woman she once was. She's a frail old thing. Last they spoke, Trixie had bought her a walker."

"Trixie?" Charlie asks.

"That's the name of the daughter, Trixie. Family name or something."

Davy glances at the old grandfather clock by the TV. It's wooden with a pendulum that swings back and forth methodically. "I'm off to bed. Sounds like the storm is letting up. I was wrong about it being a long one."

Davy is right. I hadn't noticed the strong chatter of rain had turned to a light pitter-patter.

"I'm heading up too," Charlie puts his finished plate down. "I need to sleep on the cheese. I have a lot of thoughts."

Davy gives Charlie an odd look.

"Mostly good, don't worry," Charlie says in a rush.

Harry covers his mouth with a hand to hide a laugh. I don't think Davy was too worried about whether or not Charlie's thoughts about the cheese were good or not.

Harry and I decide to follow the others up. There's no point in staying up and exhausting ourselves. I'll have a hard enough time falling asleep in a strange place, so I might as well head off to bed early.

Chapter Forty-Three

A Family Name

I turn for the thousandth time in the tiny bed that's shoved against the wall of the room. The smell of mildew overpowers my senses, and I can't sleep since I feel like I'm stuffed inside a decaying log. Davy didn't tell me whose room this once had been, but I strongly doubt it belonged to Matilda. I can't imagine her picking out mud green for her private space.

An owl screeches outside, and I twist onto my back so that I'm staring up at a water stain that has formed in the shape of a crow. It would have been more fitting for it to have been finch shaped. Maybe part of the reason I can't sleep is because today was a failure. Harry and I now know everything there is to know about Matilda and her disappearance, and even with that information, we don't have an inkling as to who killed Ken Kitson, or why someone would try to frame Matilda for the murder by placing anonymous calls about her to the police and staging matching shoe prints. Who would even know what type of shoes Matilda wears? Who paid that much attention to the comfort footwear Matilda sported around? It would have to be someone that knew her well. Peter Pinesmith, Davy's nephew and Patrick's son, had been staying with Matilda recently. Surely, he would know what her shoes looked like. Could he have killed Ken Kitson and framed his aunt?

No, that didn't make sense. The murder had happened on his property. He wouldn't kill someone on his own acreage around the same time that his father was dying. For both practical and emotional reasons, that would be rather a foolish thing to do. If only there was some way I could get in touch with Bea or Trixie. Being able to speak with either Finneas Ransom's widow or daughter would be immensely helpful.

I sit up straight and take a gulp of the humid air that hovers in the room. *Trixie and Bea.*

Davy had said Trixie was a family name. If that were so, was it possible that Bea was also a family name? Both were short for the same name. Beatrice.

I envision Beatrice's friendly face as she passes me a latte across the counter at Country Time Coffee. Was it possible that she was the grandchild of Finneas? Her thick auburn hair is usually tied back so that her soft face is easy to remember. But could she be related to Finneas Ransom? Ransom's sharp face as I had seen it in the prom photo circles my mind. Beatrice doesn't look much like Finneas Ransom. What if Beatrice's name is just a coincidence?

I lay back in bed, but another thought makes me sit back up again.

Davy had said Finneas Ransom had just about owned half of Sourwood, and Beatrice currently owns almost every business in town. What if the Ransom family had never sold that land and kept it in the family? That would explain how Beatrice came to own so much of it.

I get out of my bed. I can't lay around letting my mind cycle through endless thoughts. I need to wake Harry.

I creep into the hallway where it's dark, and I can't see anything. I'm pretty sure that Harry's room is to the right. I take a step and cry out in pain. My head smacks right into something hard and warm.

"My head!" Harry groans.

"I'm so sorry," I rub my forehead. "I can't see anything."

"Why are you two up?" Charlie says from somewhere else in the hallway.

"Charlie?" I ask into the void.

"That's what they like to call me," he says.

"I couldn't sleep," I whisper. "I couldn't stop thinking about what Davy said."

"Me too," Harry says, "that's why I got up. I wanted to get you."

"That's crazy," Charlie must have taken a step towards us because he sounds closer. "All I could think about was what Davy said too!"

"But do you think any of it makes sense?" I ask. While I can see the possible connections between Finneas Ransom and Beatrice, they seem so farfetched.

"It makes perfect sense," Charlie says.

"It does?" Harry replies.

"How else would Davy have gotten that cheese?"

"What?" Harry hisses. "What are you talking about, Charlie?"

"I think Davy might be the person buying all the cheese in town before anyone else can get to it. I don't think he actually knows the guy who makes it."

There's a long pause as the three of us stand in the dark hallway.

"Were we not talking about that?" Charlie asks.

"No," Harry snipes.

"What is all this commotion?" Davy's voice joins the conversation.

No one has a second to reply before the lights in the hall turn on. Charlie shields his eyes while Harry squints at me, his light brown eyes barely visible.

"Davy, we need to talk to you," Harry says.

"Talk to me in the morning," he bites out and turns around.

"It can't wait!" I reach out and pull lightly on Davy's arm.

Something about the urgency behind my touch makes him realize that this is serious because he stops walking and looks over his shoulder.

"What's Beatrice's last name?" I ask.

"I don't know." Davy's leathery face looks tired and worn. "Was that it?"

"No, it's not," Harry takes a step forward. He's blinking a bit more than usual, still trying to adjust to the bright light. "Davy, you haven't been the only one in Sourwood who has recently found themselves to be the target of sabotage. Emma, Charlie, and I have experienced a few things at the cabins we rented that didn't seem quite right, and now I have good reason to believe that Beatrice is behind it all."

Davy lets out a laugh. "Beatrice who owns the coffee shop in town? Why would she be bothering you three?"

"She knows we've been helping Sheriff Melville with the Ken Kitson case, and she wants to run us out of town," Harry continues. "She's been trespassing on your farm too."

"Beatrice?" Davy holds back another laugh. "The only thing Beatrice has ever done is help draw tourists to Sourwood."

"Please, hear us out," I say. "Bea and Trixie are sometimes nicknames for the more formal Beatrice. It's possible that Beatrice is the granddaughter of Finneas Ransom. Ransom had also owned a lot of property in Sourwood, and now Beatrice owns a lot of property in Sourwood. It seems like a big coincidence."

"Because it is," Davy fumes.

"Someone broke into Emma's cabin because they knew the key code, and the only person in all of Sourwood other than Emma who knew the code was the owner of the cabin," Harry raises his voice. "After we all went to bed, I looked up the company that owns the cabins we all stayed in on my phone, and they're owned by the same company as the coffee shop and several stores in town, the same stores that Beatrice owns." Harry looks

Davy in the eyes. "She's the only one who could've been bothering Emma, Charlie, and I."

Davy remains straight faced. "Even if Beatrice was related to Finneas Ransom, give me one reason why Beatrice would do horrible things after she's lived here and been a member of our community for all these years."

Harry and I are quiet. I can't think of a response. Davy is right. Even if Beatrice is related to Finneas, that doesn't prove that she has anything to do with the vandalism on Davy's farm or the death of Ken Kitson on Patrick's property and the framing of Matilda.

"I've got it!" Charlie sticks his finger in the air.

"You do?" Harry says.

Charlie clears his throat. "Beatrice is Finneas Ransom's granddaughter. She grew up hearing stories about how her grandfather's name was tarnished all through the town of Sourwood for some mysterious crime he didn't commit." Charlie makes jazz fingers to add effect to his story. "As an adult, she comes out here. Like Emma pointed out, it's easy enough, her family owns half the town. She doesn't learn much about her grandfather, and the town is nice. She continues expanding her business and then, bam!" Charlie claps his hands together loudly, making everyone jump.

"She opens a new coffee shop on the other side of the mountain, and who comes strolling in? The woman who the whole town accused her dear grandfather of murdering! She's so mad that she decides she's not going to let the Pinesmith family get away with what they've done. She starts with you," Charlie looks at Davy. "It's easy because everyone knows where your farm is. It's right next to the popular Goldfinch Gap. All she has to do is stop by here once a week and steal your eggs, or a goat, or whatever else she's been doing." Charlie waves a dismissive hand.

Davy's eyebrows pull together, and his lips thin while Harry's mouth drops open. Before either man can speak though, Charlie holds his hands up.

"When Beatrice realized Harry, Emma, and I were trying to find out who was vandalizing the farm, she must've started getting worried, so she decided to leave threatening messages and the like at our cabins," Charlie finishes with a smile. "Not bad for a guy who eats food for a living, am I right?"

"Charlie, that's amazing!" I give him a hug in excitement.

"It's nothing, really," he says bashfully.

Davy clears his throat loudly. "Let's not celebrate too early. Say Beatrice has been coming onto my farm and bothering you three at your cabins. Does that mean she killed Kitson and framed my sister too?"

"It's a strong possibility," Harry says. His jaw tenses as he thinks. "If Beatrice had been trying to punish your family, she wouldn't have only punished you. Ken Kitson died on Patrick's property, which, had your brother lived, would've created one heck of a headache for him. That's one of the reasons Peter is in such a foul mood all the time. He must be dealing with the legalities surrounding inheriting property that is actively part of a murder investigation. And, as you know, your sister was framed for Kitson's death. That would've been a good way to punish her."

"How would Beatrice have found out that Patrick and I helped Matilda escape? No one except the three of us knew about that," Davy stutters.

"Did you ever visit your sister at the coffee shop?" I ask. "If you did, Beatrice could've seen the three of you, and although she may not have figured out that you and Patrick helped her escape, she would've figured out that you and Patrick knew she had been alive and never bothered to clear her grandfather's name."

Davy shakes his head. "That's not poss—" Davy stops speaking.

"Are you okay?" Charlie asks.

"On Patrick's last birthday, I met Matilda at the coffee shop over the mountain, and we called Patrick from her cellphone. She doesn't have reception at her house. We figured it was safe enough."

"Beatrice must've been in the shop that day and overheard," Harry says. "The only question that remains is how did she kill Ken Kitson?"

"We should call the sheriff," I say.

"What for?" Davy asks. "He can't help us!"

"Last time you made the mistake of not calling the sheriff for help. We can't keep repeating our mistakes."

Davy doesn't reply. He just looks at me and gives me a curt nod.

I head back to my room where I left my phone. I'm not sure what the sheriff will do when he gets here, but I know we're about to close this mystery.

CHAPTER FORTY-FOUR

ESCAPE TO THE FOREST

E veryone is gathered in Davy's living room. The sheriff stands in the middle. He's dressed in his uniform, but he hasn't had time to shave because white stubble dots his chin.

"Anyways, we're best off if we take two cars," the sheriff readjusts his hat. "I put a call into a few stations at the nearby towns for backup, but the one nearest said they would be delayed, and who knows how long it'll take the others to get over the mountain at this time of night, especially considering all the rain we've had."

The sheriff looks around the room at us all. "Now, you're all sure that Beatrice had something to do with this murder business? We don't want to go bothering someone who doesn't need to be bothered."

Davy stands up and lets his rocking chair fall back empty. "I didn't believe it at first, but those two kids and Charlie made me think otherwise."

"I would like to point out that while I am old enough to be Harry and Emma's father, I am also young enough to be Davy's child, so I think I should be included in the phrase *those kids*." Charlie puts down the finger he had awkwardly wagged in the air to prove his point.

The sheriff scratches his head. "Anyways, I would feel more comfortable if we took my cruiser, and Davy tagged along with me. Harry and Emma are seasoned when it comes to things like this, so they can go in their own vehicle."

A snap of heat crawls up the back of my neck. Harry and I have solved murders, but I wouldn't exactly describe us as *seasoned*.

"Charlie will drive then," Harry claps a hand on Charlie's shoulder. "Emma and I don't have use of our cars right now."

"Let's not waste any time," the sheriff says. "They're calling for rolling storms all night long. We should leave now while there's a break in the rain."

It's not long before everyone has piled into their designated vehicles. The sheriff and Davy pull away in the cruiser as Harry and I snap on our seatbelts. I'm in the back of Charlie's car while Harry sits in the passenger seat up front. The fresh smell of Charlie's car doesn't exactly fit the atmosphere of the night. I feel like I'm heading out for a night on the town, not to confront someone who could be a murderer.

Charlie follows the sheriff on the country lanes as we drive under cloudy skies and past dark farmhouses and wooden fences. It's not long before the cruiser is slowing down and turning into a driveway marked by a small mailbox. The sheriff's backlights turn red as he parks his car in front of a house with symmetrical windows and a lantern path that leads to the front door.

"This must be it," Harry climbs out of Charlie's car.

Charlie and I do the same, meeting the sheriff and Davy in front of the house. The air is thick and sticky. Sweat clumps at the back of my neck where my hair is tied in a low, messy bun. While there's no storm right now, one could break out at any moment.

The sheriff knocks on the door and announces himself. A light turns on in the house, and Beatrice opens the door. Her hair is pulled back in a familiar ponytail, and she's dressed in casual clothes.

"Sheriff, is everything okay?" she opens the door wide. "Come in. I don't want you all to get wet if it starts to storm."

Something isn't right. Why would Beatrice welcome everyone into her house so easily? My stomach tightens, and I don't feel well. Maybe Harry, Charlie, and I were wrong about her. I grab Harry's hand and give it a squeeze, but he doesn't look at me.

The inside of Beatrice's house is decorated in a similar fashion to her coffee shop. There is lots of art dotting the white walls, and a cinnamon candle burns somewhere nearby. Beatrice's shoes are lined up by the front door along with her knapsack and rain jacket. Everything is neat and has its place.

She motions for us to gather in the living room down the hall where the small enclave is lit with dim lighting. Beatrice takes a seat on a white chair near the entrance while the rest of us make ourselves comfortable on her couch and remaining chairs.

Beatrice turns on the lamp next to her so that more light enters the room. On the coffee table, a large book is open to a page titled *Edible Mushrooms*. We must've interrupted a night of reading. I feel even more at fault. How could Harry, Charlie, and I have been so sure that this woman was guilty of such an awful crime? Would it be too late for me to tell the sheriff that I think I'm wrong?

"What brings you all here?" Beatrice nibbles her lips in worry. "Did something happen to one of the shops downtown? A break-in?"

The sheriff's eyes are glossy as he looks at Beatrice. "I'm here because I have good reason to believe that you may be involved in the vandalism that's been happening on Davy's farm."

Beatrice's face falls, and her eyes gather tears in them.

The sheriff pushes on. "I also have reason to believe that you may have been involved in the murder of Ken Kitson and the framing of Matilda Pierton, nee Pinesmith, for the crime."

Beatrice clamps her mouth tight. Her arms tense as she holds them at her sides.

"I believe that if I were to do a thorough search of the house, a pair of shoes matching the prints that were found at the murder scene of Ken Kitson will be here."

Beatrice looks at the floor for a long minute.

Finally, she looks up and stares into the sheriff's eyes. "I'm sorry. I'll go get the shoes so that you don't have to search for them."

She stands and leaves the room.

The sheriff stares after her in shock. Charlie's mouth is hanging open as he glances around the room, waiting for someone to say something. Davy is the only one who doesn't appear to be surprised. His face is red and his eyes are angry.

A minute passes as we wait for Beatrice to return. Out of all the reactions that Beatrice could have had to the accusation that the sheriff launched at her, the one I had not been expecting was for her to apologies and show the sheriff the evidence he needed to convict her.

Another few minutes pass, but no one says anything. I study my nails and chew on my bottom lip. Based on past experiences, I had assumed that the confrontation of Beatrice would be dramatic, but I had been wrong. People really were different in the small town of Sourwood.

More minutes tick by. Charlie continues to glance around the room while Davy stews. If I bite my lip anymore, I might make it bleed.

Eventually, Harry stands up. "Should we check on her?"

"I think that's a good idea," I get up and join him.

"I'm looking too," Davy gets up. "Charlie, you coming?"

Charlie nods his head.

Out in the hall, Harry and I go towards the front door while Charlie and Davy go in the other direction. The sheriff waits quietly in the living room.

In the entrance area, Harry opens a door that leads to a small powder room while I check out an office. There's not much in the room except a desk, chair, and computer with a large monitor.

"I don't see anything," Harry says.

I don't reply because I'm not fully listening to him. I'm looking at the shoes lined up against the door. There's an empty space where a pair could easily fit. Not only that, but Beatrice's knapsack and rain jacket are gone.

I grab Harry's arm. "She's left!"

"What?" Harry says.

Our voices carrying because Davy and Charlie appear from down the hall along with the sheriff.

"She's taken her rain jacket and knapsack," I point to the empty space near the front door. "She must have fled!"

The sheriff pushes his way to the window and looks outside. "Her car is still here, so she's on the property. If we spread out, we'll find her. Let's go!"

He leads the charge out the front door.

Charlie takes off down the driveway while Harry makes a right towards the side of the house. I don't know where the sheriff goes, but Davy must be right behind him because I can hear the two men talking to each other as they tumble through foliage and twigs.

I go left and find myself on a slick stone path that slopes to the back of the house. Grabbing my phone and turning on the flashlight app, I run along the mossy rocks, skidding here and there on slippery spots.

The stone path dwindles out and is replaced by thick mud that leads uphill towards a hiking trail. I'm not the most experienced hiker, but I've done my fair share while birdwatching. If I feel unsafe, I can always turn back.

The hill is a light incline, so I'm able to gain my footing by gripping saplings as I scramble up. Despite the climb being difficult, I've made the right decision. As I near the top, another path converges with the one I'm on, and fresh footprints appear in the deep mud. Beatrice must not be far.

Now that the ground is more level, it's easy for me to run and track Beatrice's marks. I sprint as fast as I can through the woods, ignoring the little jolts that start my heart each time my ankle twists, or I skate on the slimy ground.

Eventually, I enter a grassy clearing. I bend down and take deep breaths, sucking in the forest air. I can't keep running like this. There's a stitch in my side, and I'm dizzy. I take a step back and my foot hits a small boulder. I lose my balance and catch myself on a nearby tree branch before I fall.

A rustling in the tree line drags my attention back to the moment. Beatrice jumps out from behind a large oak.

"Don't move!" she yells, her eyes piercing mine.

CHAPTER FORTY-FIVE

IN A FOREST CLEARING

R ain drips down Beatrice's coat and pools onto her hiking boots. My heart explodes against my chest like a bird beating its wings.

"Don't move an inch!" Beatrice yells back.

She doesn't look armed, but it's hard to tell in the dark and rainy night.

I lift my foot to take a step back, but Beatrice throws her hands up.

"Please! You'll fall!" she pleads as rain continues to fall around us.

Her words surprise me, so I place my foot back where it was.

"It's dark, so you can't see, but there's a steep drop right behind that rock you stumbled on."

I freeze in place, unwilling to move and risk danger. While I don't see a weapon in sight, she's close enough to me that if what she says about the drop off is true, all it would take would be one little push for her to kill me.

"You must think I'm crazy," she says.

I clamp my mouth shut. I do think she's crazy, but if I tell her that, I might as well invite her to shove me off a cliff, literally.

She looks at me with begging eyes. "My whole life all I heard were stories about how my mother had to flee the little town she had grown up in because her father, my grandfather, had a reputation that made everyone scared of him."

"I won't lie, I don't think my grandfather was the kindest of men. He had his mean streaks. He died when I was a child, but as I grew older, I always wondered about the little town my family had once lived in. When I turned twenty-five, I found out that he had left me a trust that included all the land he owned in Sourwood.

"My mother and grandmother disagreed with me, but I wanted to come out here and make something of myself. For years, it was wonderful. Of course, I had heard about the disappearance of Matilda Pinesmith. I knew my grandfather could be mean, so I never let the rumors bother me too much. Maybe when he was a younger man, he had done something wrong, maybe he had deserved the rumors that destroyed his life? I hadn't known him well enough to be sure, and he was dead, there wasn't anything to do about it."

Streaks of water run down Beatrice's face. I don't know if she's crying or the rain is just hitting her hard.

"Then, not too long ago, I opened another coffee shop on the other side of the mountain. It was all going well until one afternoon, Matilda Pinesmith stopped in. At first, I didn't notice. The last known pictures of her were from decades ago. How was I supposed to know that this older woman in front of me was the same one who had ruined my family's name?"

"But then she came back with her brother, Davy. I wouldn't have known they were siblings except they made a call to their other brother, Patrick. I was standing right next to them when they did it. I was placing their coffees on the table while the three of them were talking on the phone. I remember thinking, this woman, this Matilda woman, and her brothers ruined my family's name. She never disappeared. She was on the other side of the mountain all this time. Her brothers and her just let my grandpa take the fall."

Beatrice takes a deep breath and swipes the water off her face. I still don't know if she's crying or not. Silence stretches as far as it can in the humid air. Then, Beatrice looks up at me.

"That's when I realized the Pinesmiths needed to know how it felt for all of Sourwood to turn on them like the town had done to my grandfather. I started with Davy. It was easy to get into his farm at night and make a little mischief. He's so unfriendly that I knew everyone in town, including the sheriff, would just write-off his complaints."

Beatrice shivers in the rain. "Matilda and Patrick were harder. Patrick didn't live in Sourwood, so I didn't know what I could do to him. I spent a long time mulling it over, but then one day Ken Kitson walked into the coffee shop, and I knew exactly what I needed to do. Ken was just a visiting hiker. He had stopped by the coffee shop and asked me for directions to Goldfinch Gap. As I was talking to him, I realized that he was exactly what I needed to make both Matilda and Patrick's life miserable.

"Ken told me that he wasn't interested in the traditional hiking trails, and he wanted to try something more difficult. I knew that the property that bordered Goldfinch Gap was owned by Patrick and not Davy because when I had first moved to Sourwood and met with my lawyer to claim my family's land, one of the cabins I was set to inherit happened to border that plot owned by Patrick, and my lawyer had given me Patrick's contact information.

"I convinced Ken to try hiking the gap from an old path that ran through Patrick's property. I told him the land was private, and that he needed to go at night if he didn't want to get caught. Ken wasn't the brightest. He agreed to the whole thing in less time than it took him to finish a small cup of coffee."

"That same night did you follow him and kill him?" I ask. My voice is hoarse, and I don't know if speaking is the right thing to do, but I can't help but ask.

Beatrice nods her head. "Ken didn't really deserve it, but I needed to find a way to show the Pinesmith family that they weren't going to live their fairytale lives anymore. I even bought the same shoes Matilda used to wear to the coffee shop and wore them that night when I followed Ken. And when it was all over, I was still able to cause trouble at Davy's farm that same night."

"And after that? You kept calling the sheriff's office to frame Matilda, and then you broke that lamp at Charlie's cabin and left those messages written in pebbles for me to find because you were worried that we would solve the case?"

Beatrice continues, "I just wanted to scare you all off. I didn't have any intention of hurting any of you. I wanted you all to be nervous enough that you would stop helping Sheriff Melville. I tried to get Sheriff Melville to let up on the case too. The day he fainted was due to me. I switched the sugar in his coffee out. Oh—," Beatrice digs around in the pocket of her jacket. She pulls something shiny out and tosses it at me. "Catch!"

I reach my hand out and clasp the small object in my right hand. It's the key to my car that went missing from my cabin.

"I didn't want to forget to give you that. After all, this isn't about you. It's about my family and the Pinesmiths. Hopefully, they've finally learned their lesson."

A dark smile crosses Beatrice's face. How does the death of Ken Kitson not haunt her? He did nothing to her family, yet she used him, his life, to make a decades old feud "even."

Several voices carry up the hill. It sounds like Harry and some others might be nearby.

IN A FOREST CLEARING

"I have to go," Beatrice says. "Be safe getting back."

"Wait!" I call.

Beatrice pauses and looks at me. I hadn't actually been expecting her to stop and turn back.

"Where are you going?"

Beatrice points up the path. "One of the old mountain trails. I've become an avid hiker since I moved to Sourwood. Don't bother looking for me. I know these mountains better than most, and I'm self-sufficient. My grandmother taught me how to hunt when I was young. It runs in the family."

Beatrice disappears into the thick undergrowth of the woods.

On the opposite side of the clearing, Davy and the sheriff tumble into view. Upon seeing them, I run over and away from the edge of the cliff. Although Beatrice never made a move to hurt me, I know I was never safe on the side of that cliff. If she had been so willing to dispose of Ken for no reason, who knows what she would've done to me had I made the wrong move.

"Where's Harry and Charlie?" I ask.

"Charlie twisted his ankle, and Harry is helping him. Have you been up this way the whole time?" the sheriff asks.

"I was up here with Beatrice. She admitted everything to me before disappearing up that hill." I point to the path that Beatrice was last seen on moments ago.

The sheriff takes a step towards the path, but Davy reaches out and pulls him back.

"What're you doing?" the sheriff asks.

"You can't go up there!" Davy gruffly replies.

"Why not? A murderer is up there! Anyways, I'm the sheriff of this town, and I don't answer to you!"

Davy steps in front of the sheriff, blocking his way. "That path leads up to the old fire road! Don't you remember, there was a root fire out that way a few weeks ago. The whole ledge won't be stable for some time, especially right after the rains we've had this week!"

A flash of lightning brightens the sky, and the soft earth below us shakes. Up the hill, Beatrice's scream punctures the air.

Chapter Forty-Six

THE ENDING

It took a while for emergency personal to reach Beatrice after the ledge of the fire road crumbled below her. She had fallen two stories and taken a bad hit to her head, but thanks to the doctors and nurses at the nearby hospital, she's going to be all right. She'll have lots of time to rest and heal from her concussion while she awaits her trial for killing Ken Kitson in jail.

The sheriff told me that when they did take her into custody, she told the officers that they didn't have anything to worry about as long as they weren't a member of the Pinesmith family. Those were the only people she wanted to hurt. I have a feeling that comment won't help her during her upcoming trial.

Not long after I returned back home, I received an invitation from the sheriff in the mail. He's finally decided to retire, and he invited me to his retirement party! I imagine his wife, Polly, is pleased now that he won't be off running around all day.

As for Matilda, she doesn't want to hide anymore. Shortly after Beatrice was arrested, she visited Eleanor. Apparently, the visit went well, and the two are working on rebuilding their friendship. I would've loved to see the reunion between the two of them, but I couldn't get time off work to go.

Unfortunately, Davy and Dottie's relationship didn't fair as well. Davy and Dottie broke up soon after we all left Sourwood. I had really thought the two of them might've found true love, but apparently Davy made a comment about Dottie's favorite news anchor, so it just wasn't going to work out. Last I checked in on Davy, he didn't seem too upset about the breakup. He said Dottie had started to boss him around too much, and he was much happier spending time in his fields with his chickens and the wild goldfinches.

The only person I haven't heard much from since we solved the case is Charlie. He sent me a clipping of his article on the Sourwood cheese a few weeks ago, but other than that, he must be in some faraway place looking for the next food he wants to write about. I hope to hear from him soon. I miss having him around. I wouldn't mind someone like him working at the magazine with me. He would help lighten the place up.

Mr. Hawking drops a huge stack of papers on my desk, making me jump. "I don't pay you to daydream, Finch!"

I hold back the groan begging to escape my lips. "Sorry, I've had a lot on my mind lately." I glance at the huge stack of work. "What is all this?"

"Your next assignment," Mr. Hawking says. "That article you wrote about Davy Pinesmith sold more magazine copies than we have in years. I'm expecting another big story from you, and I better get it soon. Oh, shoot!" Mr. Hawking pulls on his tie. "I got jam all over me again," he grumbles as he trots back into his office.

I grab my purse from under my desk and head out the office doors. It's five o'clock, and it's Friday. Harry is taking me on a picnic to a nearby lake so that we can do some birdwatching. Ever since we got back from Sourwood, our relationship couldn't be better. He asked me (officially) to be his girlfriend at a romantic dinner a few days ago. I couldn't be happier.

I spot Harry's car waiting for me by the sidewalk. I walk towards it when my phone rings. It's my mother.

"Hello!" she yells into the phone. "What are you up to this weekend?"

"I'm about to go have a wonderful picnic with my boyfriend," I reply.

Harry waves at me from inside the car. He looks cute with his button up shirt and new haircut.

"Oh, perfect!" my mother coos on the other side of the line. "Your father and I are starving! Our plane just landed, so if you text us the address, we should be able to be there soon." She hangs up.

I slip into the passenger seat, and Harry leans over and gives me a soft kiss on the cheek. He sees my shocked face and smiles at me.

"What's wrong?" he tucks a loose curl behind my ear.

I blush. "I think you're about to meet my parents."

Harry lets out a laugh. "That sounds like a great date."

We lean towards each other and our lips meet.